Longevity

By

Darrell Phelps

Copyright

ISBN: 978-1-959670-63-6

Contents

Dedication

I would like to dedicate this book to my wife, Lea, who has always encouraged my writing endeavors from the days in the Poinciana writing group through today. Included in this dedication are all my friends and relatives who have read, over time, what I write and expressed their liking of my efforts with the written word.

Acknowledgements

I would like to acknowledge my high school English teacher, Mrs. Smith, who told me I would someday amount to something if I would just learn what she was teaching. She is gone, but maybe one of her heirs will see this.

CHAPTER I

O'Hara heard the shotgun blasts, all three of them, as he walked from the coffee shop to his car. The shots came from the alley adjacent to the warehouse that was to be torn down next week. Drawing his pistol from its holsterR.G. , he set his coffee and roll down on the top of his patrol car and carefully proceeded down the alley. Just as he entered between the buildings, he heard tires squeal and race away from the far end. Running through the dark, he stumbled over a body and fell face first.

Knowing he had lost his chance to catch a glimpse of the car, he turned on his flashlight and saw a body lying on the ground, covered in blood. Besides the obvious blood, the clothes were in tatters from the shotgun blasts. Checking for a pulse, he found none and picked up what looked like a journal lying next to the body's left leg. He was looking for ID in it as he tried to call in a report. His portable radio wouldn't work right between the buildings, so he went back to the entrance he came in to make his call. Besides, his coffee and roll were still on top of his patrol car. What he didn't see was the body jerk and then rise from the ground. When he went back to get a better look, after making his report, it wasn't there. The only thing he had was a journal with blood on it and some bloodstains on the ground.

The police now had no body, just some blood stains on the ground, O'Hara's report, plus this journal. Three months later, the journal was sold at auction for the grand sum of five dollars. This is what was in the journal.

The following has been transcribed from the original handwriting.

I know you want to know just how and why I got into this particular predicament. It might not make much sense to you, but I'll try to explain. The guy T.J. and I were dealing with had no sense of humor at all. It's as simple as that. Why did he have me shot? That's not so simple and might take a while. If you care to spend the time reading this, I've got all the time in the world to tell you. At least until one of us dies. You'll probably go first, but there's no guarantee of that either. What the hell, get comfortable and I'll tell you all I can. Some things I can't, simply because I don't know right now. I do expect to learn a lot of it later. That is, if I survive this latest mess.

It all started on a hot, humid afternoon in a rice paddy in 'Nam. We had just identified the location of a contingent of VC holed up in this little village and, during the night, had surrounded it completely. The higher-ups had determined that there were only forty or so VC in the vill' and our three platoons would be enough to capture them. What a screaming mistake that was. Once the firefight started, it was obvious there were at least two hundred of them, and they were being reinforced from one of their tunnel complexes. To top it off, this was a "friendly" vill' and our illustrious leaders wouldn't firebomb the place. They did give us cover fire as we started our retreat, which wasn't anywhere near enough. Out of all those guys that started the attack, there were only seven that got away. I would still be there if it wasn't for T.J., a tall lanky guy from Tennessee. He carried my sorry ass out of there on his back for most of five klicks.

Once we were in the clear, he leaned me up against a tree and cut away my gear and fatigues so's he could see where all the blood was coming from. Most of it was coming from a huge, gaping hole in my thigh. He crammed all the bandages he had on him into the wound and reached for the medic pack. How he carried all that crap, and me to boot, was beyond my comprehension then, but I now understand. He took two of the biggest needles I had ever seen, plus some clear plastic tubing, out of the pack. He stuck the tubing onto both of the needles, crammed one into a vein on his arm and then proceeded to stick the other in me.

"I've got O negative blood. That means I can be a donor to anyone. I don't do this, you'll die. Lay quiet." T.J. said, as the blood began streaming into my veins.

As I lay there, I thought about this strange, quiet man. He had come into our platoon six months ago, dropped his gear onto the floor of the hooch, and asked which bunk was his. I pointed to the one by the door. The one we always gave to the newest guy. It usually didn't stay full long. The last new guy lasted seven days. The one before him lasted only fifteen minutes. What we didn't know was that T.J. wasn't new to war. He was just new to this one. He rarely said much, but when he did, you took it to the bank. He was a lot of fun, too. He did like practical jokes, especially if they were on him. Somehow, we knew not to pull any dangerous ones; such as firecrackers thrown into the bunker. One of the guys dropped a rubber snake from a tower on him. Once. Before the snake could hit the ground, he had drawn his knife and beheaded it in the air. He laughed like crazy when it turned out to be rubber. He thought that was so funny, he caught a real one, harmless of course, and dropped it into the shower stall of the guy who had dropped the rubber one on him. Those kinds of practical jokes stopped cold in their tracks. Shaving cream in the hand of a sleeper, and then tickling their nose, was more his style.

As I lay there, in that steamy jungle, I looked back over my life, fully expecting to die right here. I was as far away from my home as I had ever been in my life, and didn't expect to get back home to those flat lands of Texas on the Gulf Coast. I had fun growing up down there; fishing in the rivers, riding the mules my Dad worked the roads with, milking the cow, picking and eating the vegetables we grew in our two acre garden. All of us kids fought like cats and dogs, until someone else entered the fray, then we all backed each other up. No sooner than the outside threat was gone, than we would be at each others throats again. Looking back, it was a fun time.

I was born on the old homestead, in my parent's bedroom, on a cold winter night in February. By the time Gran got there, my head was showing. She helped get me the rest of the way out, cleaned me up, and laid me beside my mother. By morning, while everyone else slept, my mother disappeared into the night, taking my dad's last few dollars and his truck. The truck was found sixty miles away, abandoned, out of gas. They figured she got a ride with a passing trucker from there. No one really knows for sure, and I never tried to find out. When Gran went to the courthouse to record my birth, she told the clerk I was Jay's son. The clerk wrote Jason on the birth certificate and Gran never corrected her. Dad spent most of his time on the road with his mules, coming home once a month or so, which left our raising to Gran. As long as the chores got done, our homework got done, and not too much blood flowed, Gran sort of let us raise ourselves. She comforted occasionally, bandaged regularly, and judged disputes always with an even hand.

Gran was full-blooded Cherokee, Gramps was German-Irish. That's on my Dad's side. My mother was one fourth Choctaw, one fourth French, and half English. No one knows, or won't tell, the rest of mother's heritage. In any case, I turned out sorta olive complexioned with straight, coarse, black hair. My eyes are a sort of greenish-brown, except when I'm mad. Folks tell me they turn so dark they look black when I'm angry. I don't know. I never looked. All in all, I'm told I was a cute kid until I turned fifteen. That's when the girls started telling me I had bedroom eyes and I would hear some of the ladies saying I had turned into quite a handsome boy, destined to be a lady killer. I couldn't see it, myself. My hair was most comfortable in a flattop, and my teeth grew in sorta crooked. Not having the money for braces, they stayed that way.

Right after my sixteenth birthday, Roy and I went to a dance over in the next town. There was always a bunch of pretty girls there. Most of them came from upper middle class families and had their own cars. Roy and I were using his uncle's car, a two door Cadillac. His uncle was a pretty lenient guy where Roy was concerned. His only rules were no drinking, no drugs, and no tickets. We always obeyed the rules, simply because we would be on foot otherwise. We had always had a good time at the dances in the park. It was a covered pavilion, well protected by a grove of live oak trees, and on most spring evenings, quite cool. They always hired a local DJ to spin the records and provide the patter. He was in his thirties, but still talked like a teen. He made it a point of personal pride to stay up with the current lingo.

I had been dancing most of the night with Nancy when Al showed up with a bunch of his followers. He was Captain of the football team and very self-assured. It didn't hurt that his Pop was the local sheriff. Most of the deputies were football fans. Hell, most everybody in Texas treats high school football almost as a religion. To some; it was, is and always will be.

When football is a religion, the quarterback on a high school team is almost God. It has to be really bad for any blame for wrongdoing to stick to a high school quarterback. This night it would stick, simply because too many adults saw what happened. Besides, the school photo nut was on hand, snapping away, getting in most everyone's face with his camera. He was usually just a pest, but that night he saved my skinny little ass from jail, or worse.

Al must have had a few nips in the parking lot prior to coming over to the dance floor. When he tried to cut in with Nancy and Roy, she turned him down, telling him she didn't like the smell of his breath. Roy was prepared to back off until she told Al no. Al, being the jerk he was, shoved Roy down and grabbed Nancy to finish the dance. He laughed at her attempts to get away and only held her tighter. Roy had fallen on his knee and hobbled over to where I was leaning against one of the outer supports. When the music stopped, Nancy escaped across the floor to where Roy and I were standing. She asked if we would take her home. The adults chaperoning the dance had only seen her running across the floor, not the scuffle with Roy.

We turned from the dance and proceeded to the car.

Once there, Nancy got in the middle and I slid in beside her. Roy was getting in when he was hit from behind by one of Al's cohorts. He fell forward, catching his neck in the space between the door and the frame. I heard his neck snap from my side of the car. Just then my door flew open and Al hit me upside the head with a bottle of some kind. The bottle broke into a million pieces, scattering inside the car and out. He then swung at me again, cutting me from my temple to my jaw line. I saw a flash of light and thought I was dead, but it was only the kid with the camera.

One of the male chaperones grabbed Al and held him while his cronies scattered among the cars in the parking lot. The other men chaperoning had spread out and most of them were caught before they could get away. Someone had called the law because there were now three deputies on the scene, lights flashing. There was also an ambulance. The medical people were checking out Roy. The head deputy, Jim, strutted up to where we were, and Al started in with his lie about how I started the whole thing. Nancy, of course, repudiated what he said, but the deputy was about to handcuff us both when the kid with the camera spoke up. He told the deputy what had happened. He also told Jim he had photographs of most of what had happened and would provide them within the hour. He had his own dark room at home that was only two blocks away. Jim wanted to take the film right then, but the kid told him his brother had already taken the film home and was processing it right now. That wasn't true, but Jim didn't know that.

Just then, the medical response man came over and whispered into Jim's ear and he blanched as if he had seen a ghost. The other medical tech walked over to me, looked at my face and immediately sat me down applying a gauze pad to my face. He told me I had to go to the hospital for stitches; that it was a pretty bad cut. Jim nodded at him and I rode to the hospital in the ambulance. I knew Roy was dead, but I couldn't quite cope with it yet. The doctor that sewed my face up looked very tired, but I figured it was because he had worked some long hours in the emergency room. He told me to come back the next day to let someone look at it and re-dress the wound. My next problem was how to tell Roy's uncle about this mess.

To make a long story short, the idiot that sewed my face up left me with an ugly scar, Roy's uncle died of a heart attack when they told him about Roy, and Al wound up spending only one year in jail for his part. The jerk that pushed Roy got three years and did only six months. It was all classified as a boyish prank gone bad. When I went before the judge, it was suggested I might like the Army or the Air Force. Maybe I might like the Navy or the Marine Corps even better. No way was I going out in water over my head, and I sure didn't think I could fly. What the heck, my uncle spent a few years in the Army, and he liked it well enough to stay in the Reserves after his second hitch. The recruiter sold me a bill of goods, made lots of promises, and I wound up as cannon fodder, so to speak. More like rocket fodder, seeing as how the 'Cong didn't have cannons. Basic training was a hoot, a walk in the park compared to this, the real thing.

If you paid attention learned all you could from the old hands, you might just make it through a full tour. Some of the guys got to liking this and came back for more. A whole lot more never left on their own. They were helped out of country by the Air Force C-141 Starlifters; only those guys couldn't watch any stars. I lost some good friends that way. T.J. wasn't going to be one of them, though. I didn't know it at the time, but he had a trick up his sleeve. He even gave me a part of that trick when he gave me that transfusion. By the time the chopper picked us up, I had quit bleeding and the wound wasn't as bad as it had looked at first. I assumed I had just gotten a little hysterical and thought I had a huge, gaping hole in my leg.

The medics that took care of us in the field weren't the same ones I saw in the hospital, thank goodness. By the time I got to triage, the bleeding had stopped, and the wound was real small. The doctor had the nurse clean it up before he stitched the hole shut. He told me I would have a scar, but not as bad as the one on my face. He asked if I would like the scar on my face reduced, but I balked at that. I don't like anyone messing with my face, sorry 'bout that. Leave it alone, I was used to it. Anyway, I hobbled back to our hooch to get some rest and a cold beer. T.J. was sitting on his bunk, waiting for me to show up. He stood up and turned me around.

"We need to have a conversation, and right now. It won't wait."

"Hell T.J., let me get a cold one first." I complained as we turned around and he pushed me in the back to get me started outside.

"Got a knapsack full, all iced down. This might get a little long-winded. Three six-packs should do us."

"What about some chow? I haven't eaten all day?"

"That's in there, too. Quit your bitchin' and get your ass in gear. Ain't but so much daylight left, and there's a lot to do. Now move it!"

CHAPTER II

"A long time ago, I ran across a man from Scotland, in a different war, and a different country. I was dying from a cluster round at close range. I had so many holes in me, you could have used me for a sieve. This man had fought by my side for over six months, and we became pretty good friends. I told him of my family, my home in the hills, and of all the beauty of my part of the Blue Ridge Mountains. When the war was over, we were going to go back there and just rest for a year or so. Drink moonshine, chase women, and enjoy life. I figured we'd head out west after that. Hell, those plans went down the drain when I caught that cluster round from the Yankee cannon. He up-jumped from my side, leaped over the barricade, and wiped out that whole gun emplacement by himself. He grabbed a bag from one of the doctors in the field hospital just a few yards away, and came back to me. He drug me off into the bushes and using the same technique I did with you, gave me a transfusion. He didn't have no needles, so he used a hollow reed. He also had to use a rubber tube. Hurt like hell, let me tell you." T.J. told me, as we sat on a bunker roof in a corner of the compound. No one would bother us here.

"What does that have to do with us?"

"Shut up and listen. Here, have a sandwich and a cold beer." He said, as he threw the empties over the fence. "What happened was that my wounds began to heal up, almost immediately. I quit bleeding, the edges grew together and shortly there was only a slight scar that faded away in two days"

"This sounds like a "This ain't no shit" story in the club. That's impossible and you know it." I told him, as I ate my sandwich and drank my cold beer.

"Why don't you take off that bandage and look at your leg, if you think that's impossible?"

"Hey, it's been cleaned and I don't need to get an infection. Some of the infections you get over here don't heal worth a damn."

T.J. reached to his side and before I could say a word, he had taken that razor sharp K-Bar he carries, and cut my bandage off my leg. He flipped the gauze pad off with the point, exposing the wound in my leg. Or, what had been a wound. He cut the stitches in a single move, reached over and pulled them out. Within five seconds, any evidence of stitches had disappeared. I had no wound, just a pinkish spot on my leg, right where I had seen a huge, gaping hole, only seven hours before.

"Now, what do you have to say?"

What the hell could I say? There it was, right before my eyes. T.J. looked me right in the eyes, stuck the knife in my face, then raised up his hand and cut his wrist while I watched. The blood flowed, stopped, and I watched as the wound healed. It didn't take more than two minutes, and you couldn't tell where he had cut himself.

"Whatever scars you have now, whatever other blemishes you have, won't go away, but you'll find that any injury you get will heal right up. The amount of time it takes depends on how bad it is. That wound you got in your leg was a pretty good sized one, so it took a while. Here, cut yourself somewhere." He said, as he handed me his knife.

I never had been squeamish before, but the thought of deliberately cutting myself didn't appeal to me right then. It didn't matter, because he saw I was stalling, and cut me himself on the back of my wrist. The blood welled up, stopped, and within two minutes I was back where I had started. Not even a scar. Damn. How do you explain this to the Army? They would turn us both into guinea pigs if they found out. I would spend the rest of my life in some laboratory, bleeding into tubes on a regular basis, while they tried to find out how I did that. Not for me.

"The man I knew went by the name "Mac" but I forget his full name, and I haven't seen him since. I don't know where he is and I don't want to know. There seems to be some sort of a society where they hunt each other's heads. Something about getting the "power" from each other. One good thing about this is we don't "ring off" to them. What I mean about that is that they can tell when another member of their "society" is close by. We won't show on their personal alarm, for which I'm thankful. He said they were immortal and they could only be killed by removal of their head. I don't know if I'm immortal, or not. I haven't died yet, even though I have been wounded pretty bad a time or two. I might live a long, long time though. That canister round that hit me was during the Civil War, and I was twenty at the time. That was eighteen sixty-three, as I recall. I also haven't been hurt in the head, so I don't know."

"How on earth have you kept from being caught? I would think someone would question your birth date."

"I go to different places and get the information on someone who died at birth. It's getting easier nowadays, what with the advent of the computer. A little judicious hacking, and I'm a new man. I've had to keep up with; no, ahead of the authorities. For a while it got pretty hard, back in the forties and fifties. Communist witch hunts; you remember McCarthy?"

"You're telling me I might be immortal, or semi-immortal, just from you giving me blood? That sounds totally impossible. Hey, this could be fun. Gimme another beer. Do you get hungry? How about thirsty? Damn, I've got a million questions."

"The one thing you can't do, is tell anyone. And, yes, you get hungry and thirsty, just like you always did. You also will feel pain when you get hurt, you just heal completely, more or less. I've got no scars from the Civil War, but here lately, I can see a trace of scarring when it's real bad. Little things like that cut I gave myself, they heal up completely. The last big hit I took was in my side, a 'Cong mortar round hit close and I lost two ribs. See?" He said, as he raised his shirt for me to see. There was a very faint scar running parallel to his bottom ribs.

I could see some great possibilities with this particular talent, or was the beer clogging up the old brain path? Better sleep on it for tonight, I thought.

"Bed time for Bonzo. This has been an awful lot to absorb for one night. I think I'll think on it tomorrow. We need a lot more conversation before we rotate." I said, as I gathered up my stuff.

"Yeah, I'm sleepy, too. Tomorrow's Sunday. Maybe we can sleep late. No patrols scheduled until Tuesday. 'Night"

We waddled back to the hooch, not saying a word. I knew what I was thinking, but I wondered what was going through T.J.'s mind. What the hell, I'll worry tomorrow. I've had enough fun for one day.

What a hell of a way to wake up. The sounds of incoming mortar rounds and the staccato sounds of machine gun fire jolted the sleep right out of my head. All of us slept with our weapons and gear ready to hand, just for occasions such as this. I usually slept in my pants, too. I really didn't want to die with my shiny hiney waving in the breeze, for the whole world to see. Rolling out of my bunk, I already had my rifle in my hands, and was crawling toward the open door when the RPG (Rocket Propelled Grenade) came through the roof. No one who ever heard one of those will ever forget the sound it makes. I can't describe the way it sounds, it's something you have to experience yourself. Screaming whistle is the closest I can come.

It sounded like a secondary explosion when it came through the metal roof and another when it hit the floor and bounced into the wall. I thought I had died twice. T.J. grabbed it and threw it through the doorway into the compound. No sooner had it landed than it exploded for real. God only knows why it didn't explode the first two times, but I was grateful all the same. All of us had donned our protective gear and were preparing to go outside when the silence hit. I say hit, because it got suddenly, loudly quiet. Again I can't describe the sound, actually the lack of it, except it is overwhelmingly quiet. Strange how we speak a language all our lives, but some things can't really be described adequately.

Anyway, we checked out the outside by the simple expedient of crawling to, and then through, the doorway. Everybody in the other hooches were doing the same. A few brave souls were out walking from hooch to hooch, checking on us. It turned out to be one of our Sergeants, old "Lifer" himself. He had thirteen years in and was on his third tour of 'Nam. He had never married and had made it clear the Army was his life. Sometimes I think he liked the feeling of fear, or at least the adrenaline rush when your life is in danger. Some people cope with death by turning to booze, some with drugs, some go insane, some get on with life, shoving those experiences into a dark closet and shutting the door. A few find it exhilarating enough to continue. Those few either turn criminal and wind up either dead themselves or in prison. Some manage to find release in an ordered society like the Army and only do it as a necessary part of their job. "Lifer" was one of those.

"Alright, ladies. Gather up your skirts and come on out. The party's over for now. Charlie just hates for us to sleep in on Sunday. This was just his idea of a wake-up call." "Lifer" yelled into the compound, as he strolled between the hooches.

T.J. and the rest of the guys went outside to inspect the damage. It wasn't much, just a few holes here and there. No one died, no one got hurt. Some egos got bruised, but not much damage otherwise. I, for one, went back to bed to try for a little more sleep. It was not to be.

"Off your dead butt, we've got some more talking to do. Let's go eat before they close down the chow line." T.J. said, with a grin on his face. "I do love breakfast."

We talked all day and well into the night.

He filled me in on every time he had been "killed" and how long it took to get back to good health. Usually, not too long. The worst of the bunch was when he was working in a refinery and got burned. That took eighteen hours of excruciating pain, then itching like he had ants crawling on every inch of his body for a whole day, then a couple of days of itching just under the skin. He had learned how to block most all pain, but that time was the worst. It hadn't really hurt when he had cut me, more like a severe itching, some tingling, and then a cool sensation. He said most of the time it was like that, but once in a while, it hurt pretty bad.

"I've got five months to do and you've got six. What the hell are we going to do when we get out, T.J.?"

"I think we ought to get into the private eye business. Chase down drug dealers and rip them off. Go to work in the diving business. Hell, I don't know."

"What did you do when there wasn't a war to get involved in?" I asked.

"Mostly honest work only requiring a strong back. They don't check too far on those kinds of jobs."

"Then I'd be an asset, because I am a legitimate person. I start the business and you work in the shadows. I could pay you under an assumed name a bunch of different ways. Social security wouldn't be a problem. You'd never collect anyway. You can always be contract labor. You got any special skills you've picked up over the years.?"

"More skills than you can shake a stick at. Money, too. I always bought new product stock, such as Polaroid and Xerox when they first started up. I can't even remember all the stuff I invested in. I put it all in blind trusts payable to a Swiss bank account and take out what I need through other trusts I set up. Hard to trace me that way. No faces to go with the signatures."

"Why don't we put in equal amounts and make it a 50-50 proposition?"

"Wouldn't that depend on what we were going to do? I've got more money than you and I could spend in fifty years, even if we acted like Donald Trump. Money is just a way of keeping score for me now. The only reason I'm in the Army is that I got bored with making money and had no real friends. Tag! You're it."

"For the time being, let's talk "Lifer" into letting us take a few recon patrols on our own. We could find out a lot more if we went on our own, without having to worry about getting anyone else killed. Think he'll go for it?"

"Ask him. He's right over there." He said, pointing off to my left and behind me.

"Lifer! We got us an idea you need to listen to. Come on over and let's talk." I hollered.

Lifer ambled over to where we were, stood a bucket on its head and sat down facing the both of us. One thing about "Lifer", he never got in a hurry and always had time to listen.

"Lifer, we've got a proposition for you. We think we can get more done and find out a lot more of where Charlie is if we went on a two man patrol. We'll take enough food and water for a week but only stay out four days. The extra food is in case we get hung up and have to stay in a safe position for a day or two. We will only take knives and a couple of hand guns. I've got a silenced .22 Mag and so does T.J. We wouldn't make any noise and we think we can get a better idea of their layout. What'cha think?" I asked, as I sipped my beer.

Lifer popped the top of another beer, swallowed half of it, and did some serious thinking. You could almost hear the gears grinding in his head. I knew he was considering things: throwing out some, keeping some, and making a considered judgment about others. We sat that way for over half an hour, just sipping beer, and watching him think.

"T.J., you've only been here a little while, but I know you know more than you're letting on. You've been a soldier before but this kid has only got a little while to go and I can't figure out why he'd want to go get himself killed when he's so short." Lifer finally said, reaching for another beer. "But, if he wants to go, I'll let him if you promise to bring him back in one piece. We really need more info on Charlie and this is one way to get it. I ain't gonna tell Top you're gone unless he asks. So far he ain't ever asked."

"Lifer, this boy and I will be back in less than a week with more info than you'll believe. I don't need to watch him, he can take care of himself, and that's the God's honest truth"

"I sure hope I live up to your expectations. Hell! Coming back alive will be an accomplishment in itself. When we goin' T.J.?"

"Bout four in the mornin' should be a good time. The moon goes down about three, so it should be dark enough to leave by then and we can be far enough in the jungle to keep Charlie from spotting us by five. Whatcha think?" T.J. asked.

"Suits me, but why not wait a day so we can get supplied up and a good rest first?"

"I stay supplied up enough for the both of us and who can get any rest around here with Lifer slurpin' beer and belchin'?"

"Done and done. Let's do it!" I exclaimed.

CHAPTER III

Getting ready the way T.J. did was a snap. He had two small backpacks stowed away in his foot locker with identical gear in each one. He said we'd take these and that was that as far as he was concerned. We sat opposite each other and applied makeup to each other's faces to match the jungle motif fatigues we both wore. Then we took off anything that would jingle, stowed all our personal gear in his foot locker, taped our dogtags so they wouldn't rattle. We even put makeup on our hands and arms up to our elbows, but kept our sleeves rolled down. We then made sure we had our pants bloused properly into the tops of our boots, spent some time taping magazines side to side, bottom to top for quick change in case of a firefight. All that done, we each ate a LRP (Long Range Patrol) meal, went to the latrine and did our business then returned to grab some shuteye before we took off.

I thought T.J. could wake up on his own like I do, but I had to wake him up at four, just like his mama did. Grabbed his foot in one hand and guarded with the other. He came up ready to take on whatever had touched him. In that split second, his eyes fixed on me,

I knew we'd come back in one piece. He snorted, swung his feet to the floor and motioned me to follow him. Latrine time again, then over to the RVN tents where we cadged some soup from the cook. Once we got away from their tent, before I could get even a taste of the soup, he spilled his on me in several places, smeared it around, and then motioned for me to do the same. DING! The reason dawned on me. We smelled just like the Vietnamese, not like Americans. The soup obliterated any G.I. odor we might have on us. It would probably attract every bug in the jungle, but Charlie wouldn't find us with his nose. Learned something new today. My daddy had always told me when you quit learning, you might as well dig your own grave and pull the dirt in over on top of yourself because you were just taking up valuable space needed by a human being.

T.J. and I picked up our backpacks from our hootch and skirted through the shadows over to Willie's post on the perimeter. Willie never saw us until we stepped into the backlit opening of the officer's tent and T.J. softly whistled. Once he saw us, he waved us on towards him with just a small gesture against his pants leg. Swiftly crossing to his post through the mottled shadows, we came up behind him and T.J. lightly touched him in the small of his back. Willie sat for a moment, then nodded his head toward his left. We slipped quickly into the trench to his left and made our way to the barbed wire surrounding the camp. I lifted the bottom wire carefully, just high enough for T.J. to get under and he held it up with his foot while I made my way through. Once that was done, we crawled slowly to the jungle, which was forty yards away. Once there, we stood up and blended in with the trees and shrubs for at least two minutes before T.J. tugged at my sleeve. Following his finger, I could see two 'Congs sitting behind a machine gun adjacent to a large tree. We crouched, silently made our way through the brush, and got the hell out of Dodge.

Our four-day foray in the wilderness lasted five only because we got caught in a tiger trap on our way back. How the hell we missed it was; it was on the same path we had gone out on. The 'Cong had dug it while we were checking out what they had around the camp and they are good at hiding things in the jungle. Even a hole in the ground as big as this one was. I was just thankful they hadn't filled it with pungee sticks. That would've hurt like hell. Once we fell through, they didn't take long to come get us out and make prisoners of us. We didn't last long as prisoners; just one day. They decided we would be better off dead, so they shot both of us, and left us in the jungle.

It was very strange, feeling the life slip out of me; but even stranger, feeling it jump back in. Good thing the 'Cong had left, 'cause I grunted pretty loudly. T.J. was already waiting on me. He has had more practice than me at this dyin' stuff. He just grinned, hauled me up with one hand, and mouthed "this way", pointing to the East. I didn't even hesitate, I just followed like a little puppy, only quieter. It only took up four hours to get back to camp, just before sundown. Willie was back on his post, so we threw a couple of small pebbles at him 'till we had his attention. Once he peered toward us, I waved a small white hanky over my head. Willie stood up and scrunched his fingers up like he was squeezing a ball. We crawled our way through the small, shallow channel we had left from and made our way back under the fence.

Once inside the compound, Willie grinned, slapped us on the back, and continued to guard the camp, never taking his eyes off the jungle. Willie would make it out of here, if caution alone would do the trick. Seven more days and Willie will make like a bird and fly home. He is taking no chances with his short time status. He even has made extra armor from pieces of discarded, torn up flak jackets for his legs, crotch and butt. Willie be one cautious man. He wants to raise those kids of his himself. According to the photos Willie carries, Diana Ross is a dog compared to his wife. More incentive to get back home in one piece.

Once we had cleaned up, got some chow and a couple of beers in us, Lifer sauntered over to talk to us. We were sitting on a pile of sandbags waiting to be filled, enjoying the sunset as much as we could.

"What you boys find out; out there amongst our little friends?" Lifer asked, adjusting the sandbags to his butt.

"They're scattered all along the river and have very little in the way of supplies, as best we can figure. That will probably change this week when their re-supply comes down from the north."

"How do you know that?" Lifer asked, reaching into T.J.'s bucket of beers.

"Overheard one of their radio operators while he thought he was all alone in the jungle. The supplies are coming down the trail on the Cambodian side, then by river boat next Sunday. The stuff is supposed to get distributed from the junction of the little river and this one, 'bout fifteen klicks from here."

"You sure 'bout that? This ain't no fairy tale you're telling me to make me think y'all really went out into the brush?"

T.J. handed Lifer the little satchel he had brought back with him. When Lifer opened it, out fell an ID book, an ear, and some carbon copy paper.

"That's his ear, his ID book, and the carbon. Couldn't take the real paper, or they'd know it was not just him deserting." T.J. said matter-of-factly.

What he did with the body, I can't say. I didn't see it when he got the stuff.

"I'll pass this up to H.Q. and see what they make of it. Sure hope they listen this time. If they'd listened last time, we wouldn't be here in this god forsaken hole." Lifer said as he tossed his empty into the recycle bin they gave to the villagers weekly.

T.J. and I just looked at each other and both knew H.Q. would dawdle like they always did and the re-supply would get through if they were left to their own devices. I'm sure the same thought went through each others' minds at the same time because we both got up and headed for our own supply dump to see what they had we could use on our own.

The supply Sgt. had plenty of C-4 and we found some outdated illumination rounds scheduled for destruction in addition to two cases of 40MM grenade buckshot rounds. We also located a roll of det cord the Seals had brought on their last foray and conveniently left behind.

The supply Sgt. only wanted a few items we had liberated from the 'Cong, such as a flag and a bugle for not noticing us hauling our booty off. We were happy to trade; we were going to take care of a problem H.Q. would lose in the endless arguments over who would get the credit for something we were all needing. Damn, it seemed when someone got promoted to Division, they forgot all they had learned beforehand. The troops in the field became pawns in their race for more rank, more credit and power.

Top took the info from Lifer and didn't ask where he got it. Top would probably say he got it from the Montaignards so no brass would investigate. Top let all of us operate out of left field once in a while as long as it didn't cause him too much grief. Don't get me wrong, he cared about us. He would back us to the hilt when push came to shove unless we were dead wrong, then he'd hang us himself. Top had twenty eight years in and knew how to work the system. He said he was going to give it up when he rotated this time and move to Florida. He called it "The home of the newly wed and the nearly dead" and said "I ain't no newly wed, that's for sure".

By the time H.Q. sent word back to us to re-verify our information, it was Saturday. We knew our operation was on and so did Lifer and Top. When Top told Lifer, he made sure we were within earshot, then walked back into his tent for his after lunch siesta. He didn't want to see us leave. He didn't know we were leaving after dark, but he wouldn't look to see what we were up to this afternoon either. He knew damned well we had stashed stuff in different places around the camp, just in case. Nonetheless, he had to be blind to certain things, to save his ass in case our operation blew up in our faces, so to speak.

The afternoon dragged on and on, it was so humid and hot. We had to go in circuitous patterns to keep Top from seeing what we were "borrowing" so's he wouldn't get in a bind. That made for more, smaller trips to get it all in place. When we asked Willie if he'd like to join in, he just grinned, snorted and said something that sounded like "Fool, don' you be yankin' my chain." I thought it was funny, even though Willie didn't. He was due to spread his wings Tuesday morning and make it out on the Freedom Bird. Can't say as I blame him for not seeing the humor in my joke. If I were that short, I'd be covering my butt up too.

When night time came, we were ready. A couple of the other guys wanted to go along as far as the river to provide back-up, but we convinced them we didn't need any help. Besides, if one of us got hurt, it would be a big problem explaining. We gathered our stuff up and Willie let us out the same way he let us out before. We were carrying a bit more stuff this time and had to go a little slower. By the time it got full dark, only a quarter moon was showing and it was already half way down. Just right, we thought, for getting our things set up on the river junctions before the supplies got there. This was going to be a blast, if everything worked right.

Getting through the jungle was no problem for us with the quarter moon helping and we made the fifteen klicks by the time the moon dropped below the canopy. We found a log big enough to support us and our stuff as we crossed to the other side where we had to tie off the end of our support cable. We got that done, hid the end so they wouldn't stumble on it, and strung our C-4, 40MM grenades and the illumination rounds on the cable to give the best pattern for the spot we figured they would unload their supplies

As the sun broke pink in the east we had everything ready, were in position to fire it off and already had reconnoitered a way to "get the hell out of Dodge" when the time came. The time was right now. We could hear the putt-putt of the small engines the 'Cong used on their river boats in the distance. Once they got loaded up, we would "pop 'em good" as Willie was wont to say. It didn't take long for them to get the stuff onto the boats. They had lined them up side by side and used a long plank to load all three boats at once. These boys were good about getting large quantities in these long narrow boats without sinking them. Sinking them would be our job in a minute or two. Just as they were pulling the long plank back to the bank, T.J. whacked 'em a good one. He twisted the handle on the little Hell Box he had brought along and the blasting cap set the det cord off, which set off the C-4 we had strung on it under the boat loading area. All three boats came out of the river in two pieces, bow and stern pointing downward, goods flying everywhere.

What was left of the personnel were milling around on the bank when the illumination rounds blew apart above them, scattering burning magnesium down on them like a stream from a shower head. It wasn't pleasant to watch, so we took off down river on our planned escape route, carefully skirting the booby traps we had already set up with the 40MM grenade rounds. We had set them up with trip wires and aimed them to slow down any pursuit. We didn't hear a one for at least thirty minutes, but we know at least one of them worked. He screamed loud enough to be heard for two counties. We had no idea whether any of the others worked. We made much better time leaving than coming, skirting places we thought traps might have been set.

Top didn't ask any questions of us when we strolled back through the camp, he just looked at us and when I gave him a thumbs up, a smile started, then disappeared. He couldn't officially sanction anything we had done, but I believe he admired our work. Hell, we admired our own work. Willie was grinning from ear to ear because it gave his flight out a better chance of making it. Less men to shoot at him and less ammo to fire at the chopper that would take him back to the land of the big PX. He was a happy man, to say the least.

The days drug on as always, but T.J. and I made the most of the nights, harassing the enemy every chance we got. We even went so far as to buy ourselves oversized decks of playing cards with nothing but aces of spades in them. The 'Cong were a superstitious lot and the ace of spades was a death card for them. Leaving one at a site we had hit spooked the crap out of them and made them wary of working during the hours of darkness. We had the advantage of night vision goggles; cumbersome as the battery pack was, it made our job so much easier when we could see them but they couldn't see us on nights with no moon.

If either of us got hit, we just laid up till it healed and whacked them all the harder the next time out. Pretty soon, they caught on that if they stayed at least three klicks away from our camp at night, we wouldn't bug them. Then they got stupid and planned a big meeting with some of their advisors in one of their camps only five klicks away. We decided to do something about that and discussed it with Top and Lifer.

"You think you can get a Spooky or Specter to join in the fun?" we asked Top, once he understood our plan.

"I believe I can get a Specter, if you for sure can spot for him." Top said.

"Spot, hell! We'll ring 'em for him. Can you set it up on time?" T.J. asked.

"My middle name is "On Time".

Top was as good as his word. He had confirmation of a Specter on site at nine p.m. and T.J. had our signal worked out by the time the confirmation call came through. We were to light off a Willie Peter (white phosphorous) grenade on the four corners of where we wanted them to hit. We had just eighteen hours to get them in place and ready to set off. We were going to use timers but Lifer had a better idea. He had access to radio control modules for model planes that would serve as ignition devices if the Specter could transmit on a specified frequency. One phone call confirmed they could and off we went to get the WP grenades in place.

We already knew where the camp was located and about how big an area it covered. What the hell, if we obliterated a little extra countryside, it really wouldn't matter. The place was already pretty well torn up. Three of the WP grenades, complete with timer, were easy to place; but the fourth one was a real bitch, so to speak. It had to be placed at a bend in the river, and the only way to do that would be to put it in a tall tree immediately on the bank of the river. Somebody had to climb the tree, set the grenade and get back down without being spotted. Guess who got elected?

I didn't mind climbing the tree, you see; I just didn't relish doing it in the dark. My night vision is nowhere as good as a cat's, so I would have to work by feel much of the time. T.J. wanted to start a diversion on the other side of the camp so I could climb the tree in daylight hours, but I vetoed that. No sense in firing them up ahead of time. Let them think they are all alone in the jungle this once.

Dark fell and I started up the tree. A few spiders, snails and such, but no real problems. It was after I set the grenade I ran into trouble. I hadn't seen the python on the way up, but he had seen me. I probably matched the size he liked in monkey meat, so he ambushed me on the way down. When he sank his teeth into my arm, I knew I was in big trouble. He had already anchored himself with his tail and that damned python was rapidly engulfing my body with his. My K-Bar was in a shoulder sheath, hanging handle down, or I would never have gotten it out in time to cut off his head before my other arm would have been trapped in snake coils bigger than my leg.

T.J. almost fainted when that snake body fell on top of him, still writhing. It took the both of us, prying with our K-Bars and cutting jaw muscles to get that damned head off my left arm. Healing quickly was a blessing in this case as the snake had sunk his teeth in to the bone. Thank goodness the pain didn't last long, as it was excruciating, to say the least. It itched like hell most of the way back, but the sight of all that jungle being shot up comforted me no end. The raids and attacks would stop for a while, at least.

Top and Lifer bought the beer, Cookie supplied the pizza and all of us supplied the camaraderie that followed the pasting of that meeting. A patrol went out the next day and counted bodies. They came back with a count of over three hundred as best they could tell. It was a mess, they said. There were even some automobiles, or what was left of them, scattered throughout the area. It had to have been a bigwig meeting, if they had come in cars.

The rest of my tour was dull and boring, only occasionally interrupted by moments of terror and pain Even knowing I wouldn't stay dead, the pain of dying by the methods usually used by the 'Cong was not fun at all. The pain of being shot was minor compared to being blown up by a booby trap or being impaled on bamboo stakes. Nope, no fun at all.

We, T.J. and I, were taken out of field ops and put in charge of training the green beans on how to stay alive long enough to be useful. That turned out to be one sweet job and got us a lot of contacts back

Stateside. They tried to get us to stay longer and I did—one month to match T.J.'s rotation date. When they came at us both with fresh extension papers, we both told them where to put them. That cost us a week on K.P. before rotating. Who cared—we weren't getting shot at during the day and we both slept well at night in those lovely air-conditioned barracks.

CHAPTER IV

After we mustered out, T.J. and I went to the required courses to get our "Private Eye" licenses from the Sate of California. Upon graduation, we incorporated according to the laws—or should I say "I incorporated" since T.J. didn't legally exist. Anyway, we set up a business and almost went nuts waiting for our first customer. It took two months and three days for the first money—legal money—to roll in the door. He rolled in on a wheelchair smoking a cigar that would make a skunk run. I had to open the window and turn on a fan to keep from choking.

"I got money and I need a job done. You up for it?" He growled.

"Depends on the job. What you have in mind?" I asked from the window.

"I need to find out who's selling drugs to the kids in Franklin High and stop 'em." He growled again. "They've already killed two kids and my son is in rehab from some bad drugs. He's in a coma and may not live. Whatever it takes to get rid of these animals preying on kids is what I want."

I didn't really have to think about it, but I took a little time anyway. Getting rid of drugs could be a bit hazardous, but hey, that's what T.J. and I specialized in.

"The fee is $500 dollars up front, which will buy you a week of time, but no action. That's a different ballgame altogether." I said.

"If you can find out who they are, it'll be worth $500 dollars to me. If you can get rid of them, it would be worth a lot more." He growled, as he reached into his pocket and pulled out a wad of bills big enough to choke a horse—maybe an elephant.

Peeling off five bills, he laid them on the desk and riffled the rest to let me see they were $100's or bigger. I saw a lot of zeros on some of them in the brief time he riffled the bills.

"I don't want you to do anything you believe to be illegal, I just want them not to sell drugs anymore, however they get persuaded. If you can accomplish that, this roll will stay in this office. I won't pay you by check." He growled once again.

I was beginning to think this guy was part bulldog the way he growled. I picked up the bills and examined them closely. They were legitimate. Part of the "Private Eye" course was on how to spot phony money.

"Deal. Do you want to sign a contract? All we have to do is fill in the blanks." I said, as I pulled one out from my desk drawer.

"Not necessary for my part. I had you guys checked out by some friends on the force and two of them knew you from the Army. Besides that, I can't find out anything on T.J., your silent partner. Past his Army days, he only existed for a couple of years, then the trail disappeared. I also have some friends in IRS. No concern of mine whether he's legit or not. I've got guys working for me that couldn't stand up to an INS investigation." He growled. "Whoever he is, is your problem. I just want the drugs stopped—permanently if possible."

"We'll see what comes down after we look into it." I said with a grin.

He filled me in on what he knew about where and when the drugs were being sold, complete with hand drawn maps. I told him we would start this evening. He nodded and rolled back out the door. I was curious as to how he negotiated the stairs in that contraption, so I peeked as he left. He was being carried, chair and all by the biggest man I've ever seen. He had to be seven feet tall and must have weighed three hundred fifty pounds. He looked back at me and grinned as he went down the stairs. They got into a limo and left heading west. That's as curious as I got.

T.J. came out of the other room and cocked his head as he looked at the maps the man had left. He picked them up and compared them to a map he had pulled out of the file cabinet.

"You didn't even get his name, did you?" T.J. asked.

"Nope. Didn't get a contract either."

"Damn, ain't this fun work?" T.J. laughed.

After a nice Italian meal, complete with a bottle of red wine, we set off to find our drug dealers exactly where "Growler" had said they would be. Growler was our name for our client, seeing as how we didn't know his real name anyway. The dealers on the street were teenagers or very young adults. We needed to find out who their suppliers were, so we waited in the shadows and watched. About eleven that night, we found out. They were cops. Damn, I hate dirty cops.

We got the number of their car and as soon as they left, T.J. followed them on a motorcycle while I went back to the office to look at whatever I could find on our computer. It's amazing what is available on a computer with the right programming these days. The programs set us back four thousand dollars, but they were going to prove to be worth more than that in the next week.

By the time T.J. got back it was after three in the morning and I was bushed, but T.J. was fired up.

"There's more of them in on this. Six at least, but I think we'll find more if we stay on them for a while. That two met up with four others in a warehouse near the docks, and split up when they left. The new ones I followed went back to their station house and I quit for the night. We need another scoot for you and some radios they can't hear. I'm gonna get some single side band C.B.'s for us, handheld of course, so we can follow two sets of cops at a time and see how big this operation really is."

"Whoa, whoa, T.J. I don't have a license for a motorcycle and besides that, don't know how to ride one." I exclaimed.

"You will in two days. Trust me, it's as easy as riding a bicycle, but you don't have to pedal." He told me, grinning all the while.

I could see T.J. was going to have fun, but I wasn't so sure I was going to have any. I was greatly mistaken; the motorcycle he bought me was a blast and following those doper cops was as easy as falling off a log- - -mostly.

The motorcycle T.J. bought me wasn't exactly a motorcycle- - -more like a moped. To start it, you had to pedal it like a bicycle and if you had to get up a steep hill, you'd best get a running start. It was quiet, though. I left it running a few times to get closer to see better and had a hard time finding it in the dark. The kids the cops had selling the dope were dumber than dumb and the cops were so confident they were immune, they generally failed to watch their back at all.

The C.B. radios worked great. We had worked out a transfer code to let each other know which channel and which side to work so we couldn't be followed from channel to channel just in case someone overheard us by accident. We changed channels on the quarter hour like clockwork and if we suspected we were being listened to, we used the transfer code and jumped. I doubt anyone knew what was happening even if they overheard us. Besides the channel jumping and side switching, we used our own brand of language- - -a mixture of English, Spanish, German, Japanese, Thai, Vietnamese, Lao, Italian and Philippino. Example: Kibegan, Polezei didi sinestra. Ein pooying undt due poochai. Translation: Friend, Cops going left. One female and two males. OK, OK. It is silly, but it works for us.

Within three days we had identified seventeen youngsters and eleven cops in on the deal. The problem now was what to do about the whole mess. Which cops could we go to with the information to bust the set-up? Were there more cops in on the deal higher up or was it just the ones we knew about? It seemed likely someone above them might be in on it because of the constant changing of the cop's territory. They moved around too much to not be allowed the freedom. T.J. decided to try to find out how and why they were constantly changing areas.

Posing as a freelance writer, T.J. went to two different stations and found out cops liked to talk, especially to reporters. They were led to believe they were gong to be the focus of a story about life as a cop in the big city. They ate it up and blabbed everything he wanted to know except why the floaters were floating. Nobody seemed to know anything about how to float from area to area. It finally dawned on T.J. that nobody knew about the floating except the floaters. They were covering for each other without the knowledge of the dispatcher. It wasn't evident how they were informing each other until he spent the next night following one of the sets of cops. They were using cell phones instead of radios to talk to each other and keep the information from the good cops. We both felt stupid for not seeing it sooner. We were using hand held radios and they were using cell phones.

"I feel like a dummy for not seeing it before now." T.J. said ruefully.

"Well, go buy a scanner that can hear cell phones and we'll be one up on them again." I said.

"It's not that simple. Digital phones can't be picked up on a scanner, only analog phones can. I'll bet even money they're using digital."

"Get a scanner anyway. At least we'll have their phone numbers and maybe screw up some of their operations."

"Here I am being a dummy again. Of course we'll have their numbers. All the signals between towers are analog and we'll have their cell numbers. Numbers is my downfall. Numbers keep giving me trouble. I can never get my numbers straight."

"Oh, shut up. Your brain is caught in a loop and it's driving me crazy. Go get a scanner and write down the numbers. Then the numbers will stop buggin' you and me both."

T.J. shook his head and took off on his motorcycle- - -the real one. His scoot had an eleven hundred c.c. dual pot motor; was water-cooled and shaft driven. He'd had better mufflers put on it to make it quieter, but it would still run like a scalded ape.

Me, I just sat down and began to make out a plan of surveillance that would give me the most eye time on **my** sets of dirty cops. I had gotten myself a nice camera with a long lens and was using four hundred film. It wasn't the finest, but it was fast enough to get their faces in dim light situations, such as alleys and doorways. Words wouldn't be enough to bust them; I needed something on film. Video would be nicer, but I didn't know if I could get close enough to shoot video.

T.J. showed me the scanner he'd bought and I bounced my problem of getting close enough to shoot video off his noggin. The scanner worked fine, but nothing came of any of my ideas other than a consensus that they wouldn't work. We'd just have to make do with still shots for now. It was better than nothing, T.J. said. I suppose he's right, but I still would love to get some of it on video.

As darkness fell once again, we were off on another surveillance run and hopefully would finally get enough good photos to identify the whole bunch.

Just when everything was going so well, somebody cranked up the fan. I was busily taking pictures of two of the bad guys from atop a brick wall when my collar went backward rapidly. Of course my body followed and I landed flat of my back staring up at a dark blue uniform with a cop inside it, staring down at me. Or should I say scowling? He wasn't pretty from this angle, so I started to roll over and get up. Error! He stomped on my arm and damn near jerked it out of socket. I loudly protested and shouldn't have. He then put his size one thousand boot on my throat and I stopped protesting immediately.

He took the radio from his belt and called his station to report his arrest of me for unspecified charges. I say unspecified because I didn't hear too well with the blood pounding in my brain, but it did register he was talking on a radio rather than a cell phone.

Reaching down from the mountain, he yanked me to my feet and sat me down on the little bench by the wall.

"Just what do you think you're doing? Don't you know this is private property and you're trespassing?" He demanded from less than six inches away in a very loud whisper.

I couldn't talk, so I handed him my card from my front shirt pocket and tried to let him know which name on it was mine.

"So who you spyin' on? He demanded in that loud whisper of his.

I still couldn't talk so I wrote on the little pad I had in my other shirt pocket- - -***Drug dealers and dirty cops***. Showing those words to him would either get me killed or helped.

He squinted his eyes at me and looked puzzled. That's when I showed him yesterday's batch of photos I was carrying. The longer he looked at the photos, the redder he got in the face.

"You told anybody else about this?" He wanted to know.

I shook my head and wished I hadn't. It made my neck hurt.

"My name's Robert and I want to help. My father, grandfather and two uncles were cops. They were the best men I knew and they hated what dirty cops do to the rest of the force. Whatever I can do to help, just name it".

"First thing you can help with is to let me walk off some of your excess. You don't realize how strong you are. I've got sore in places I'd forgotten I had."

He gently helped me to my feet again and we walked and talked a bit as I worked the kinks out and my body did its healing thing. He didn't see any of that as it was all internal, but this was one of the times I was glad I could heal up fast.

"Listen, I can help out more if I cover you while you do your spying thing, can't I?"

"Not really. We work best alone."

He laughed and said; "I wouldn't say that. I just walked up on you. I wasn't trying to be quiet. You need to listen better if you're going to be in the sneak business."

"Let me run it by my partner and see what he has to say before I commit to anything, OK?"

"You need some help; all the help you can get." T.J. said from the shadows.

I jumped.

"See, you didn't even hear me coming. Robert had his hand on his gun until I handed him my card and you didn't even see that. We need to work on your attention span."

Well, I could see the handwriting on the wall from this conversation. We had another partner, at least on this particular job. I did need someone to watch my back. I'd never been any good at keeping my mind on more than two things at a time.

Having resigned myself to another partner, I set about getting some real info on the guy. As far as I could check out through the computer, he was who he said he was. He had left out the fact that two of his sisters were detectives in another city. Maybe it was a sibling thing.

Night fell and again we were off to make another batch of photos if we could find someone to follow or get ahead of. Robert did what he said he would do and kept my back covered. I had finally gotten my photojournalist friend to loan me his videocam that would make tapes in the lowest of lights. Hopefully, we could get the dirty cops on video tonight, too.

Locating the dealers was easy; they were brazen as could be with cops for protection. We followed a pair of them to a pizza parlor near the waterfront and got some good video of an exchange of money for drugs in the parking lot. The dealers and cops both were getting extremely lackadaisical about where and when they did their deals. Better for us, right?

CHAPTER V

I had just put the videocam into the saddlebags of my moped when I felt something hard against my ribs and a rough voice sounded in my ear.

"Why you takin' videos of my friends?" Whoever it was rasped.

"I'm making a documentary about night life on the waterfront for the local PBS station." I said as I slowly started to turn around.

I was grasped by the collar and prevented from turning by the simple expedient of being thrown into the power pole my moped was chained to.

"Hey, what's your problem? You want the tape, you can have it. It wasn't all that good anyway. I thought I was getting tape of women and it was only some cops busting some juvies chops about the curfew." I lied.

I reached into my outer jacket pocket to get the blank tape I always carried there when my lights went out. I didn't hear a thing; the lights just went out. I found out later the joker shot me in the back with a silenced .45 auto. The slug went through my spine and then through my heart before exiting my chest into the power pole. Not a good way to end the night.

T.J. and Robert both jumped the guy and had him on the ground when the cruiser rolled up in response to Robert's call on the radio. T.J. tried to stop Robert from calling, but was a bit late. Now his problem was how to delay all the others while I healed up enough to get on my moped and get away.

Luckily, the new arrivals got in a dispute with the cops from the pizza parlor about who should be covering this. Their squabble gave me time to struggle to my feet and get my moped headed downhill before I cranked it up, three blocks away. I hoped my getaway had gone unnoticed but I still used evasive tactics. After making some very rapid alley and driveway ins and outs, I knew they would never get on my tail before I could get completely healed. T.J. could find me with the CB or simply wait at the office for me to turn up. If Robert were smart, he'd keep his mouth shut and let T.J. do all the talking.

They found me at the office, lying down on the couch watching an old movie on TV, with not a care in the world showing on my face.

T.J. said Robert was a quick learner, and had kept his mouth shut. T.J. had *not* explained where I had gone after being shot in the back. He let *me* explain to Robert how it worked. I threw in a small demo, consisting of a small cut along my forearm. Robert was amazed as he watched the blood stop flowing, the edges of the cut pull together, and only leave a small red scar line. Within a few seconds the scar line began to fade to my natural skin color and within two minutes, there was no evidence of my arm ever being cut.

"Did I really see what I just saw? What are you, some kind of alien/human cross? No natural human can do that." Robert sputtered.

"No, I'm not an alien/human cross. I've just become a very fast healer through an accidental blood transfusion a long time ago. I'm unable to explain it better than that. I can't really tell you how it came about, either, because I'm not absolutely sure I understand what happened to me." I lied.

"Boy, that trick would come in handy as a cop." Robert said, as he leaned back.

"It could get you into more trouble than you know. Unless you really think about how you might use it, it can make you a bit reckless. To this day, I'm not real sure what it would take to put me down permanently disabled or even dead. I really don't want to try and find out, either." I said.

T.J. hadn't said a word during any of this and at this point got up off his stool and left the room. I assumed he was going to do something to convince Robert not to try to find out how I got like this, but he had only gone to get a soda. He had forgone beer for the best part of this month but I don't know why.

"Robert, we're going to get these dirty cops and try to set it up so you get the credit. We'd just as soon nobody even knows we do this sort of thing. That OK with you?" T.J. asked.

"Whatever you want, just as long as we get them and kill their drug ring." Robert replied.

"I figure to set them up for a sting of our own and get as many as we can at one time. The good guys can figure out the rest, because you know someone is going to sing to get his sentence reduced. They always do. This ain't the Cosa Nostra, just a bunch of bad cops gone real bad." T.J. said as he sipped his soda.

We sat up late that night formulating and discarding many plans but finally came up with one all of us felt would work. T.J. was in the background again this time along with Robert while I became the Judas Goat. I would start with buying small amounts, progressing up to the kilo range in less than a week, whereupon I would show up with a large wad of cash and demand to see someone up the line who could sell me up to ten kilos at a time. I had a very rich clientele base and they demanded I keep up with their partying or they'd find someone else to supply them.

I figured I could make three or four buys from one of the dealers and then demand to go higher up the chain. As far as we knew, this loose group of cops was the whole chain, but it wouldn't hurt to try and see if they're in this alone.

As it turned out, after the second buy, one of the cops came to me and wanted the meeting. He said he could get me fifty kilos at a pop if I had the cash. I showed him enough to make his eyes bug and he set the date and time. I agreed to come and bring enough money for fifty kilos on Friday night in the alley across from Kelly's Café and Deli on Thirty-second Street.

Now that the initial trap was set, the rest of the plan went into effect. Robert would mastermind getting IA (Internal Affairs) in on it to collar the bad cops as soon as they made their move. T.J. was going to be covering us from the rooftops and make sure it wasn't too bad an ambush. He had some heavy stuff he'd use if it got wicked.

Friday night came and I stepped into the alley carrying my case of money, ready to make a drug deal. I tucked my journal into the inside pocket of my jacket over my heart. I had been writing down most of what had happened in my life, starting with 'Nam. I thought of it as a possible fiction story I could sell later on. No one would believe it was a true story.

The previous was in the original journal bought from a police auction. The remainder is from a later journal brought in by one of our associate agents.

As I swaggered down the dimly lit alley, I caught a glimpse of movement near one of the overhanging stone facades and assumed it was T.J. Out of one of the doorways hidden in the shadows stepped the figure of a man I believed to be my dirty cop. I kept on, knowing I was backed up by the best. Imagine my surprise when I finally could see my adversary. It was Robert.

"Yes, it's me, Robert. You thought I was one of the good guys and all along I have been getting my cut by protecting the "Group" while they ran the business. We decided to get more money the easy way---take it from you. Hand it over and we won't hurt you." Robert said.

I knew that was a lie, because I could see the sawed off shotgun hanging under his trench coat. Robert gave me a slow wink and then raised the shotgun. Damn, he *was* going to shoot me and take the money. I dropped the case and tried to turn and run. Too late—the shot hit me square in the back and I went face down onto the slick bricks. Robert walked up to me, used his toe to turn me over and shot me again directly in the chest. By that time I was so far gone, I didn't feel a thing. As I faded, Robert kneeled down to pick up the case and whispered "Sorry, I'll explain later."

From further down the alley, three other men stepped out and one patted Robert on the back before they all got into the black car that had just pulled up. Tires squealing, they left my body lying there on the damp bricks. O'Hara tripped over me trying to get the license number of the speeding car and failed. He did pick up my journal, which ended at Kelly's Café and Deli.

By the time O'Hara got through with his radio call, I was up and gone. I didn't notice my journal missing until later when I was changing clothes. It didn't concern me too much, as I figured it got torn up with the shotgun pellets when I got blasted. T.J. came in while I was changing and glumly sat down.

"I thought he was on the square, didn't you?" He asked.

"I think he still is. He didn't shoot me in the face and whispered he'd explain later just before my lights went out. Maybe he was between a rock and a hard place. Let's wait and see." I declared as I sat down to put on my socks and shoes.

"OK, but if it turns out he's swapped sides and is drugging, I'm going to take him out, gangland style. Damn, I hate drugs and the people who deal in them."

"Whatever, T.J.. I just want a good meal. Every time I do this I come up starving. Wonder why that is?" I mused.

"You ever think about how much energy it takes to rebuild even your skinny little ass?" T.J. said, laughing. "I have to eat twice as much when I get tore up."

"Replacing that much lard must take at least three pigs." I said, dodging the soda can he threw at my head. Good thing it was empty.

"You're right, lets go eat. I'm hungry, too."

We made our way through the evening traffic to our favorite barbecue joint and found ourselves a table. Sometimes it takes a while to get the right seats. T.J. and I have both become paranoid about having a fast escape route and keeping things in sight. Important things, such as the entry and exit doors, possible ambush windows and/or new employees acting funny.

When Janie came over to take our order, she sat her tray down on the table, which wasn't usual for her. She usually turned it upside down and used it as a support of her order checks. Unsmiling, she took our orders and when she picked up her tray, there was a small folded paper lying on the table. I spilt some sugar making my tea sweet and swept the paper into my hand in order to read what was written on it.

"IA is in the ring. Got recruited and had to prove myself. First encounter-2AM-be there."

"IA is dirty too?" T.J. whispered.

"Seems so. What's this first encounter mean?"

"Doofus. He means the first time he met us."

"Oh, yeah, right." I sputtered. I am a little slow sometimes.

Janie brought our food and pretended she didn't know us all that well. T.J. spotted a guy in brand new jeans, a striped pearl snapped shirt and a bandanna around his neck sneaking peeks at us over the seats. When Janie refilled our tea glasses, she left us another note that read—*IA in the drugstore cowboy outfit.*

Janie earned a double tip that night. The regular twenty percent we usually gave left on the table and a century note T.J. slipped into her pocket on the way out when he picked up his usual doggy bag. He flirted with two other waitresses on the way out so it wouldn't seem he was picking on Janie. No use in making Janie a target for the bad guys.

We sat around and watched movies on TV until one-thirty. We approached our rendezvous point from separate directions and skirted the area looking for traps. We found none. Robert was sitting on the brick wall waiting for us.

Without preamble, Robert began, "When I approached Detective Brown in IA, he took me into a private room and during all the talking, he kept leading me to talking about money. I smelled a rat and started complaining about low pay—wishing I could make more. The more we talked, the more I complained. Eventually he wanted to know if I really wanted to make BIG money and was I persnickety about how I made it. One thing led to another until I was in, more or less. I had to make the pick up for them on Friday and there was no way to let you know what had happened. They had a man on me the whole time. He even spent Thursday night at my place. Sorry about shooting you, but if I hadn't they'd've shot me and I can't rejuvenate. I tried to stay away from your face; did I make it?"

"Yes. No real harm done. What now? How many more in this ring?"

"I don't know yet. I figure it'll take at least a month before they really let me in on the rest of it, if then. It may take much longer. How far should I let it go before we bust them?"

"Who you going to bust them with? IA is in on it—who else is dirty? Damned can of worms is what it is. Wonder if the Chief is dirty too?" T.J. said. "Keep us posted on whatever you can find out. Are you going to keep using Janie as a messenger, or what?"

Nope, Janie was a one-time deal. She's too easy a target. She's a friend of my sister's and I didn't plan on using her at all. It just worked out that way, for this time. Here's a pager that belonged to my little brother. I reactivated it just for this situation. I'll call you and if I don't get a call back within ten minutes, I'll re-call with a new number. I'll be using pay phones. IA has access to phone records and I don't want them tracing to this pager."

"So far, so good, said the man who fell off the roof as he passed the tenth floor. What happens if they catch you? I don't like any of it. I'd rather quit while we're ahead and can the worms we know. With your testimony, we can put them away for a long time." T.J. declared.

"Sure, even if they bring up the fact you shot someone; where's the body and was it a real body or just a decoy? O'Hara can't testify that it was real, just that the blood was real. I'm with T.J.; it's too scary for you to keep this up. I'd rather keep the marbles we've got rather than risk your health. Yeah, yeah, risk is part of the job, but not this much risk. You might as well paint a bullseye front and back and carry a sign "Target practice here!"

Robert grinned and let out a sigh of relief, "Boy, am I glad you said that. I was willing to try this but the other night spooked me no end. Let's find someone in the department who isn't dirty and get rid of this bunch of dirty cops"

T.J. slid off his spot on the wall and spit out his toothpick before saying, "Nope. We're going to the State DA and lay the whole thing in his lap. We don't know who's dirty besides the ones we have pictures and video of, sooo---let *him* put the worms back in the can. That's why he makes the big bucks, our big tax bucks."

"Suits me, says I." I chirped.

"You betcha'." Robert said as he slid off the wall. "I've got the early shift so I'm heading for home to get a little shuteye. See you guys tomorrow."

We waved good bye to him as he slid his body into his sports car. Cranking it up and turning on the lights, he headed home. We turned to head for home when the night lit up and the explosion almost knocked us down. Turning quickly, we caught sight of parts of Robert's car sailing through the air, still burning from the gasoline. He must have had a full gas tank, there was so much fire. We both stayed until the fire trucks had the fire put out, but there was no hope at all. Parts of Robert were scattered for fifty yards in every direction, according to the fireman we talked to.

Trudging down the street to our respective rides, we both said nothing, but I'll bet our minds were running in the same direction and it wasn't pretty. Detective Brown was high on my list of next for reprisal. Whether or not he set the bomb, he was definitely part of it and innocents besides Robert could have gone up in flames, not to mention homes. I was thinking of some dirty tricks to pull when T.J. spoke up.

"Yeah, I've been thinking of how to get even and I really think prison in the long run is going to be best. I have some contacts within the prison system and I think life will be one different stage of hell on a daily basis for these creeps when we get them in there. Now the only problem is getting them in there. Can we do it with only the drugs? I don't know, but I'm for sure going to try."

"If we can get them in prison, I'm all for it. If not, there's always later, right?" I asked.

Just as we reached our bikes, a spotlight hit us full in the face and a voice told us to raise our hands above our heads.

"Just what are you doing in this neighborhood at this time of the mornin', laddies?"

O'Hara boomed at us.

"You know what we do, Patrick. We were surveilling a local Romeo when somebody's car blew up." T.J. said as he put his hands down.

"Malarkey, I say. You know damned well it was Robert's car that blew up and he was here to meet you. I saw two of IA's rats messing with Robert's car this afternoon, but didn't ever see Robert to tell him. I left a note on his steering wheel, but I think the rats took it off. I was on my way to tell him in person when his car blew. You boys have to go to the State DA and blow the whistle on them. I'll help if I can; if nothing more than testifying about the car."

"O.K., I'll get in touch with the State DA in the morning and let you know what comes down." T.J. said as he straddled his bike.

Patrick turned off his spotlight and said he'd drop by our office at ten in the morning, as he didn't get off until eight A.M. That would give him time to clean up, get a bite to eat and change clothes.

The next morning, T.J. called up the State DA and made an appointment to see him on Monday at eleven o'clock in his office. We ordered some breakfast from the deli on the corner, ate and were cleaning up when Patrick O'Hara knocked on the office door. I let him in.

"Well, boys, did you get a meeting set up with the State DA? Do you have all your ducks in a row? Is all your evidence in order and available to take up to the capitol?"

"Sure thing." I said. "It's all in that filing cabinet in the corner, all packaged up and ready to go."

T.J. sat his coffee cup down on the desk and swiveled back around to face the desk as I sat down on the corner.

"Are you going to be available when we need you to testify, Patrick?" T.J. asked.

"Anytime you need me." Patrick said as he reached inside his jacket and pulled out a pack of cigarettes and a lighter. He lit his cigarette, returned the pack to his pocket and pulled out a nine-millimeter pistol, slipping the safety off as he drew it out. "Sorry boys, but I need the money to pay for my wife's cancer treatments. I've already mortgaged the house to the hilt, and I just can't get any money anywhere else. This is going to earn me two hundred thousand. Sorry."

Neither T.J. nor I made a move as he shot T.J. twice in the chest, and then shot me once in the forehead. T.J. had slumped in his chair and I fell off the desk, blocking the file cabinet.

I was getting good at this reviving. Before Patrick had gotten my body moved from in front of the cabinet, I could see again. I was still pretty much paralyzed, but my eyes had cleared up enough to see that T.J. was fully cognizant and was moving his hands. Patrick couldn't see behind the desk from in front of the filing cabinet.

Patrick pulled the thick envelope out of the top drawer and saw the videotapes we had put in it. He then pulled out the folder marked "Dirty Cops" and was leafing through the reports we had written up by the time I sat up and T.J. stood up. O'Hara didn't even notice that we were up, he was so absorbed in reading the reports.

T.J. punched O'Hara hard in his left kidney and when Patrick straightened up, he punched him in the jaw with a wicked left hook. Patrick moaned and then fell to the floor, out cold. I slipped handcuffs on him and we then looked at each other.

"Just how the hell are we goIng to handle this? We sure as hell can't tell anybody he shot us and we didn't die. Damn,damn,damn!" T.J. groused.

"Tell you what—let's take him up into the mountains, strip him down to his underwear and leave him there. If he's anything of a woodsman, he can get back to civilization in a couple of days. Let him figure out what to say to his bosses, both clean and dirty." I said, as I blindfolded him, trussed up his legs, and rolled him up in the office rug.

T.J. thought a minute, grinned and nodded his head. We carried him down to the service elevator, rode down to the garage and put him in the trunk of my car. In less than two hours, we were almost to the top of the hiking area we both liked. It would take Patrick the better part of a day to get from there to a paved road on his bare feet, then another half day to any civilization. That's after he got out of the rug and if his feet held up. We weren't worried about anyone tracing us through the rug; it was a common type, carried by at least three different major stores.

Patrick grunted when we dropped him on the ground, a lot less than gently. I stayed behind and brushed the first fifty feet of our tire tracks into oblivion and then got into the passenger's seat and buckled up. If you ever rode with T.J. you'd pray for all the safety devices you could find. He drove like the proverbial madman. I don't know if he ever had an accident, but I sure didn't want to be in the car with him if he ever did. Even knowing I would rejuvenate, it still spooked the hell out of me to ride with T.J.

We saw no one on the way up or on the way down. It was sort of odd not to see any traffic at all, except that it was hotter than hell and probably most of the hikers were staying in the malls. Worked out good for us, in any case.

By morning, we had cleaned out our office, erased all evidence of who had been there and headed for greener pastures. Patrick O'Hara had our names, but that wouldn't do him any good at all; they weren't our real names. It was T.J.'s original idea, but it had served me well. Both of us had three or more different ID's we could use. Identity wasn't a big problem, now that computers were so prevalent and T.J. was such a good hacker.

CHAPTER VI

By the next weekend we had moved to Texas and set up another shop in Texas City, just south of Houston to start all over again. It had been so much fun we thought we would continue with the same modus operandi. Two detectives who would work cheap, wreak terror in the hearts of the drug dealers and help people as best we could by not charging much. T.J. and I loved our work, if you could call it that. Getting paid for having fun is not really work, but we had to do something to try and spend T.J.'s fortune. It was getting so big it was hard for him to keep up with all the accounts. The local charities were happy with all the anonymous donations of cash they were getting and the people they were helping sure enjoyed it.

As usual, for a while no one knocked on our door or rang our phone. It got so boring we decided to hit the local precincts and see if we could scare up a drug dealer or two. T.J. had been a cop once or twice in his long life and had no trouble talking their language. He found out where the cops hung out after work and where they ate.

He even went so far as to buy one of the little coffee shops, but kept the same people running it at a better rate of pay than they had been making. He spread the word that if you showed a badge, your meal was half price and coffee was always free. The rumor he spread along with it was that he was from a long line of cops back East, but wasn't physically able to do the job.

The cop started trickling in a few at a time and when they found out the food was even better than before, but at a better price, the floodgates flew open. The waitresses were paid well by the hour and even got their tips, too. Whether or not T.J. reported the tips I never knew and didn't care. We had hired a bookkeeper to take care of that end of the business. I was responsible for ordering the food and keeping up with inventory. Shoot, I had no idea what I was doing, but learned quickly the cook was good at that so I let him do it and double-checked what he did.

As time went by, the cops began to ignore the fact we weren't cops and talked to us about what was going on throughout the city. I had a pretty good memory and would write notes after they left and at night T.J. and I would sort it all out. It seems most of the drugs were controlled by two ganglords; one from the East Side and one from Galveston Island.

We assumed the one from Galveston Island was bringing in his stuff in by boat and distributing it the same way. There were so many pleasure boats and so much commercial traffic; the Coast Guard couldn't keep up with it all. We were going to give them a hand in locating the routes and carriers if we could infiltrate the gang. T.J. let his hair and beard grow, bought a boat suitable for running drugs and started letting the word out in the right circles that he was in the market.

It took another month for someone to approach him about buying a couple of kilos of coke at a good price. They met at the docks and sat on the fantail of his boat with rods as if they were fishing. People did that a lot in that particular marina. From time to time one of them would reel in a fish and toss it back just to keep the charade going.

"You know I'm new in the business down here. I had to leave New Jersey a while back to let the hunt cool down, so I thought I'd do something to keep my hand in while my cousin takes care of my works in New Jersey. What the hell, maybe I'll just stay here. The fishing seems to be good and there's lots of money to be made if I can find the right supplier. You him?" T.J. asked.

"I can get whatever you want and as much as you want, whenever you want it. My Jefe lets me take care of the distribution in this area. If I do good, he'll expand my territory and up my cut." Fillipe said with a smile. "Tell me more about your ops in Jersey. You know I have to check you out before I commit myself."

T.J. wrote a number down on a napkin and said, "Call this number, mention that you're a friend of Bolivar Juarez and they'll tell you anything you need to know."

"Who is Bolivar Juarez?" Fillipe asked.

"It's a code word to let my cousin know he can talk to you. You don't say the right words and he'll deny knowing who I am. Do you want to use my cell phone? It's digital and can't be listened to. Call him right now, if you like."

"Sure, I'll talk to him."

T.J. handed him the phone, he dialed and when T.J.'s cousin answered, it was with a New Jersey accent. I'd spent some time in New Jersey so I sounded authentic. T.J. had programmed his phone with a code that would make that particular number ring on my cell phone at the café. I had to get up from talking to some of the cops and move to the office to talk to Fillipe. It just wouldn't do for the cops at the table to hear me laud a drug dealer's operation.

After some few minutes of conversation about the weather and such, Fillipe mentioned Bolivar Juarez and asked if I could tell him about T.J.'s business. I told him it had grossed around seventeen million last year, which was slow because of the State D.A.'s dogging him. It usually ran over thirty million, but the D.A. had popped six of his best distributors and was currently trying them. We felt sure they would walk as soon as we took care of a few witnesses' monetary problems.

That seemed to allay Fillipe's fears and we chitchatted some more about boats, the Coast Guard and the DEA. After he hung up, I broke out in a cold sweat. I hoped I had done well enough and wouldn't know until T.J. called me back. A cold beer cooled me off and I relaxed enough to turn on the television and watch an old movie I had seen bits and pieces of, but had never seen the whole thing through. When the phone rang, I knew it was going to happen again.

"It seems I'm in for fifteen kilos tomorrow night. I have to meet them at the channel buoy at nine P.M. with no lights and alone. And, oh yeah, thirty thousand dollars in unmarked bills; no consecutive serial numbers and nothing larger than a fifty. Sound like a set-up to you?" T.J. said with a grin in his voice.

"Might be, but we can get around that. Let me find my scuba gear and wet suit and we'll set them up for a fight for first place in Davy Jones's locker. I know it's in one of the boxes in the storage shed. I'll go look right now." I said, after I guzzled the rest of my beer.

"I'll locate some firepower and meet you at the boat in two hours, OK?"

"Great. That'll give me time to make sure my tanks are working right."

Two and a half hours later, I showed up at the boat to find T.J. stowing gear and boxes in the after well. I lugged my scuba gear over the side and undid the aft line while T.J. loosed the fore line. He had already warmed the engine up and when he turned the key this time the big four hundred cubic inch Chrysler engine began it's deep throated, muffled roar. T.J. eased the throttle forward and we slowly growled our way down the channel to the open bay. Nothing was said as we made our way between the pleasure craft, barges and fishing boats until we reached the open water of the bay.

Once in open water, T.J. eased the throttle forward a bit more and the boat seemed to leap to on plane. With just that little tweak of the throttle, that Chrysler engine seemed happier and we were headed out at a clip I had never traveled before on water. Glancing over at the gauges, the RPM's were only two thousand, but our speed was sixty by the speedometer on the dash.

"Just how accurate is that speedometer, T.J.?" I asked, as my hair, what was left of it, blew straight back and my eyes watered.

"It's a little slow, according to the Coast Guard radar. Right now, we're probably doing a little over seventy. Not real sure." He said, with a grin.

It was a good thing the bay was calm. Even so, what little chop there was made for a very bumpy ride. About the time I started to feel comfortable, the throttle got shoved up another notch and the ride smoothed out. I think it was because we were only hitting the tops of the waves. When I glanced at T.J., he was grinning ear to ear. He looked at me and, using his fingers told me we were doing ninety.

He leaned over so I could her him over the roar of the engine and the wind whistling in my ears and yelled, "What're you afraid of? You can't die, you know."

Like that made me feel better. I still white knuckled the bar I was holding on to until he chopped the engine to idle once again. He looked at his watch and said, "Seventeen minutes from the dock to the buoy. What I'll do tomorrow is have the guys in the next slip set off some fireworks just as I leave the dock. You'll be here at the buoy and when the fireworks go off, you can count down seventeen minutes to my arrival. Suit you?"

"How'm I going to get out here. It must be four miles in a straight line from the beach. No way can I swim that far. I'm too out of shape."

"It's called a rubber dinghy and an electric trolling motor. We don't have time to try it today, but you can go fishing tomorrow morning and see how long it takes you. You fish on the way back in so you don't look suspicious to anyone."

"So lets hang my gear on the buoy now and I can sink the dinghy tonight when I get here."

"Let's do it." T.J. said.

We rigged my gear, encased in heavy plastic, to hang below the buoy on the seaward side. T.J. had his firepower set up the same way. He had brought for my protection: one Mac10, one Korean War vintage forty-five caliber M-1 Grease Gun, six hand grenades and two White Phosphorous smoke grenades. There was enough ammunition for both guns to fight a prolonged fight. What the hell, it was only money and it just might get well spent. We'd find out tomorrow.

Early the next morning, just after sunrise, I went fishing in my little rubber dinghy. It took me only two and a half hours to make it to the buoy, even thought I had a head wind and a rising tide. It should be between tides when I left for the buoy tonight, according to the tables in the newspaper. Just the same I would leave early enough to overcome unforeseen circumstances. We had a light lunch, T.J. and I, before we set up the money in a briefcase and stashed it on the boat. He would stay with it until it was time to leave and I got to go fishing again.

I took off at six that evening and was within a few hundred yards of the buoy when I spotted a trail of bubbles off to my right. I cut the motor, even though it made little noise and paddled my little dinghy toward the bubble trail. It, too, was headed for the buoy. I made it first and tied off so I would have both hands free. The trail of bubbles ended when a black rubber encased head popped into view adjacent to my dinghy.

"Hi. You fishing, too?" I queried.

When he raised his hand out of the water holding a pistol, I whacked him on the head with my oar and grabbed him by the air tank and yanked him to me. He was carrying a sealed plastic bag with a MAC 10 in it with four extra magazines. I took the rope off the front of the dingy and tied him up, leaving just enough to keep us tied to the buoy. I cut his gear off him and dropped it overboard. His fins were better than mine were, so I kept them. Dragging up my scuba gear and wet suit, I dressed myself and eased my way into the water.

I had tied whatshisname into the dingy facedown and now I turned the dingy southwest, set the tiller for straight ahead and sent him off to be by himself. Maybe when the battery ran out, he might be able to paddle back to land if he had any idea where that might be. Not my worry.

By now it had grown dark and when I checked my watch it was twenty minutes to nine. The fireworks should start pretty soon. I finished off a small bottle of water, tucked it into the bottom section of the buoy housing when I saw the fireworks in the sky. I also heard the roar of an engine behind me in the distance. I knew it wasn't our boat by the sound. It got closer and then I could hear that Chrysler's roar. My hair stood on end at the back of my neck, because the other boat would get here before T.J. If they found me instead of whatshisname I could be in deep trouble.

The new boat pulled up and stopped maybe thirty yards away and shined a flashlight toward the buoy. What to do, what to do. Do I show myself or hide.

"*Todos listo, Carlos*?" Came the question.

"*Si*." I answered.

I heard them chuckle and then the light went out and we waited for T.J. to show up.

T.J. pulled up to the buoy and tied his boat off, then they pulled up alongside him and tied their boat to his, bow to stern.

"I've got the money if you've got the goods, Fillipe."

"Let's see the money and I'll show the goods." He said

"Mine's on the deck, open. Do the same with yours." T.J. countered.

A few bumping noises and a light shone onto T.J.'s deck while T.J. shined his on theirs.

"Pitch the bag third from the top and second from the right over so I can test it." T.J. said with that grin in his voice. Damn if I don't think he likes a good fight.

"Pitch over the second from the bottom and third from the left bundle of money so I can check it."

A thump in T.J.'s boat and a thump in their boat told me the exchange had taken place. T.J. sat down and went through the test of their product while they perused the money bundle. After everyone was satisfied, they exchanged briefcases and they untied their boat and started their engine. Once they had turned around and were parallel to T.J. again, Fillipe reached into the small of his back and pulled out a pistol, aiming it at T.J.

"I would like my goods back now, Senor." Fillipe snarled.

"Don't think so. I paid for this stuff and I think I'll keep it." T.J. snarled right back.

By this time I had my M-1 Grease Gun out and aimed right at them. I had inflated my Mae West enough to keep my head and shoulders above water. Fillipe could see me now because the wind had pushed me from behind the buoy and both boats.

"Orita, Carlos." Fillipe yelled.

"Carlos went for a boat ride into the darkness a while back and I don't know if he can find his way home again." I said, as I cocked the M-1. "I think you boys best go on home with your money and leave us be with our merchandise."

Fillipe fired at T.J. and I heard the round hit him hard. My M-1 one did the talking for me as it stitched a line of big holes through Fillipe, his cohort and their boat. The engine whined and stopped grumbling, the two men in their boat went down, and their boat began to sink. I swam over to their boat as the gunwale began to slosh in the slight chop and grabbed the money case, which they had the foresight to close. I reopened it to check it was there, and pushed away from their boat as the stern sank. In only two minutes, their boat had sunk to the point the bow was the only part still visible. Heaving myself into our boat, I checked T.J. out. He was lying there on the bottom of the boat with a grin on his face.

"Have a good time?" He asked.

"Damn, you recovered fast." I said, as I began to take off my gear.

He unsnapped his jacket, then his shirt and showed me the flak jacket he was wearing, That nine-millimeter slug was still stuck in his jacket, flat as a pancake. "Those boys will never learn to stop using those nine millimeters. They think a lot of bullets are better than one good one. You stopped them and sank their boat and I'll bet you didn't even use up half your magazine, did you?"

I checked, and sure enough, I had used only twelve rounds out of my thirty round magazine.

"Lets go home, get cleaned up, stash our stuff and go chase some women. What'cha think about that?" T.J. said with a laugh.

"How do we explain about Fillipe, if someone should be so bold as to ask?"

"Let's ride that dragon when it catches up to us. Right now I want a thick juicy steak, some good fries and a cold beer, not to mention some dry clothes."

Not having a reputation as a party-pooper, I had no intention of starting now. I got the rest of our gear from below the buoy and we headed back into port.

The wind had picked up, making the swells about two feet high, so we sort of waddled our way for most of the trip. When we got behind the seawall, it smoothed out and we made better time.

After cleaning up the boat, and ourselves, we got into T.J.'s new car, a candy apple red Viper. He had a thing for speed. His boat was way over powered and so was his car. I wondered just when he would get an airplane and how fast would it go.

"Steak and Ale okay with you?" He asked, as we left our little three-bedroom cottage.

"Sure. I love their peppered steaks. And they have good beer on tap, too." I replied, as my head slammed against the headrest. T.J. also has a heavy foot.

We parked at the rear of Steak and Ale in a spot far away from other cars. T.J. wanted no dents, dings or scratches in his pretty red car. Can't blame him, myself. It just tears me up to find a mark on my car from some careless jerk.

Walking the short distance in spotty light soothed my nerves until T.J. nudged me and nodded toward a Cadillac limo coming toward us. We kept walking, but unbuttoned our jackets for quick removal of our handguns. We both had procured concealed weapon permits along with our licenses as P.I.'s. The limo stopped a few feet short of us and the back door opposite us opened. One man got out and signaled for us to come over. Neither of us could see if his other hand held a weapon, but we complied nonetheless.

The rear window on our side silently slid down and a dark skinned man with a goatee just beginning to gray politely asked us if we were "Ucant Hyde Investigating, Inc.". We both nodded at the same time. Seems the longer we're together, the more we act alike and in unison.

The man introduced himself as Carlo Montez and asked if we had a few minutes to spare.

"Why don't you join us for dinner and we can talk all you like?" T.J. asked with a sweep of his hand indicating Steak and Ale's front door.

Carlo directed his driver in Spanish to park the limo and wait while he talked with us. The man on the other side of the limo didn't speak, but closed the door and waited while the limo drove off. T.J. stared at the other man as he stood with his hand inside his jacket. Carlo turned and told the man to wait there, by the power pole, until he returned. I saw the faint blush creep up his face, but he didn't say anything. He only backed up into the shadows by the pole and never took his hand from inside his jacket.

T.J. and I really got his goat when we turned out backs on him and walked away without a backward glance. I could see him in the mirrored window of the restaurant and he almost pulled his hand out of his jacket, but kicked the power pole instead. He assumed he had scared us. When we didn't show fear it upset him, poor fellow. Carlo preceded us and had already procured a table in the corner when we got inside.

Polite chitchat preceded the drinks and the meal. Neither Carlo nor we wasted time talking once the steaks arrived. Coffee was ordered after we finished and Carlo finally got down to business.

"I understand you have a very fast boat. Do you race it or is it just for entertaining the ladies? Carlo asked.

"Sometimes I race the clock and the ladies do like the wind in their hair. I have even used it to go fishing, so to speak." T.J. replied.

"What kind of fish do you catch when you go fishing?" Carlo wanted to know, as he sipped the hot coffee.

"Mostly greenbacks, but sometimes pesce de oro. Either is fine with us. We like the finer things in life." T.J. said. "Sometimes we trade or catch for other things of value. We do a lot of trading."

"We must do some trading sometime. Here is my card, call me tomorrow and maybe I can trade you something you'd like. I tried to do business with Fillipe Monteverde, but he seems to have disappeared. It appears he had a boating accident and they have found no bodies as of yet. The Coast Guard found most of his boat a long way from shore, but no evidence of flotation gear. Poor man, he wasn't much of a swimmer I'm afraid."

"We both swim well and my boat is manufactured not to sink. I don't think we'll have that problem. What we may have a problem with are poor businessmen." T.J. drawled. "Some of them think cheating your customers is quick, easy profit. That kind of thinking can cause permanent damage, don't you think?"

Carlo's left eyebrow raised slightly, then his face broke out in a wide grin. "I do believe you could be right. Filllipe may have been one of those types. He stole some of my product and I knew he was trying to peddle it here, but I couldn't locate him. I now believe I never shall. I think he "took a powder", so to speak. No great loss except for the missing product."

"Would you like to retrieve the product or, better yet, find the money from the sale? We two are in the finding business in addition to the restaurant business. I believe we might be able to help." I said as I handed him our card.

Carlo read the card and laughed. "A nice play on words, your business. Did you have a price in mind for the work?"

"Twenty percent of either the money or the product seems a fair price." I said.

Carlo thought that over and replied, "Twenty percent of the money or ten percent of the product is more what I had in mind. Ten percent of the product can be worth more than you think, if you find the right buyer."

"But that would put us in the position of finding a buyer for a product for which we have no distribution network. That would mean a large expenditure for recruiting, warehousing and the like. For that kind of outlay, we would need the profit from extra ten percent." I said

"I can provide the network and warehousing for you at a small percentage, say one percent. That way, your profit would be nine percent which is still more than twenty percent of the money." Carlo replied, as he lit a cigar.

"Let us think it over and tomorrow we can meet again." T.J. said.

A waiter came toward the table and haughtily began "There's no smoking in---" and immediately turned away when Carlo removed his glasses. The Maitre De looked startled when the waiter returned and whispered in his ear. They both left hurriedly.

I paid the bill at the register, T.J. left the tip and we left the restaurant. Opening the door into the muggy night, I noticed Carlo's man was still in the shadows and still had his hand in his jacket. I excused myself and headed for the car while T.J. and Carlo waited for the limo to roll into position to retrieve Carlo.

As the limo rolled by, I darted into the shadows behind Carlo's man and waited for him to move toward the limo. When he did, I circled my left arm around his neck and pulled back as I slid my right hand inside his jacket on top of his. Before he could react, I had his pistol in my hand and he was leaning back against me. I moved backward, keeping him off balance, all the while putting pressure against his throat. Once I had his pistol, I let go with a leftward twist, which caused him to stumble and fall to his hands on the pavement. Carlo and T.J. didn't even notice, as the limo was blocking their view.

When the driver stepped out to open Carlo's door, he stopped with his jaw open. Carlo looked over the limo and saw his man getting up from the ground and me unloading the Glock. I dropped the magazine into my left hand and jacked the round out of the chamber as I rounded the rear of the limo.

"You really need to find better trained guards. This one is strong, but only between the ears," I said as I handed Carlo the semi-auto pistol.

The man I had just disarmed snarled as he rushed me from behind. I waited, listening to his steps and just as he reached me, stepped backward and drove my left elbow into his solar plexus. When he stopped, I turned to my left, hooked my forearm under his jaw and drove my bent right knuckles into his windpipe. He fell to his knees, choking and I hit him hard on the forehead with the heel of my left hand. I heard his knees pop as he fell backward. He passed out from the pain and just lay there, still gasping.

"Sorry, Carlo. I didn't mean to put him out of commission. I only wanted to keep him from hurting me." I said, as I rolled him over on his side, so he wouldn't strangle.

"Juan, put Santo in the back seat. I'll ride up front with you." Carlo said to his driver.

Juan scurried to do as he was told before the explosion of temper he was expecting came.

Carlo looked at me, then at T.J., who was just standing there, chewing on a toothpick. "On second thought, we can meet tomorrow to discuss a contract at your original offer. I like the way you handle yourselves. I think we can do much business together."

Carlo extended his hand for both T.J. and I to shake as Juan folded Santo into the back seat of the limo. Carlo got into the passenger seat in the front, closed his own door and Juan slammed the back door to hurry into the driver's seat. The limo tires squealed slightly as they left the parking lot.

"What the hell prompted you to kick Santo's ass so hard?"

"Carlo and his ilk operate from a position of power through fear. I just thought I should show them we weren't afraid of his soldiers and to prove to him we were better, faster and smarter than the average bear."

"I do think you got Carlo's attention and certainly Santo's. If he recovers from his evening and Carlo keeps him around, I would grow eyes in the back of my head, if'n I was you." T.J. said as he unlocked the doors to his Viper.

We slid into the seats, buckled up and I started praying again. I was surprised when T.J. kept it under the speed limit the whole way home. I supposed he was thinking, as he had an odd expression on his face the whole trip. Opening the garage with his remote, he pulled up to the door, but didn't drive in.

"What the hell is that?" He asked.

Lying across the entrance to the garage, in the expansion joint, was a clear tube. We couldn't see the ends of it from the car, so we got out, leaving the lights on for better light.

I went right and T.J. went left. Following the tubing all the way to the wall, T.J. could see his end went inside and curved back against the wall. My end terminated at the wall with the end bent over itself and taped down. I yelled to T.J. what I had found and he motioned for me to come to him. We could both see that the tubing was taped to the wall in the corner and followed it with our eyes to then see where it reversed itself against the ceiling to disappear above the garage door.

Carefully making sure we didn't step on the tube, we went inside and I got the stepladder to look above the garage door. Neither of us wanted to lower the door in case whatever was there might activate. I climbed the ladder to see what I could see. T.J. handed me a flashlight and I shone it into the darkness above the door.

"Claymore." I whispered.

"No need to whisper, it can't hear you." T.J. whispered back.

Ýou absolutely sure it isn't also sound activated?" I whispered back.

"Nope" He whispered. "Is it connected to the door in any manner?"

I shook my head and continued to search the darkness for anything else unusual. All I could see was the tubing, the Claymore and what appeared to be a battery pack with a small electronics package taped to the battery, all sitting on a small shelf attached to the front of the garage.

After I got down, I told T.J. we should take care of this ourselves and not get the bomb squad involved. No need to hurt anybody else. Besides, I was pretty sure this was Carlo's doing and I planned to give it back to him. He agreed.

I retrieved the package from the shelf while T.J. detached the tubing from the floor, wall and ceiling. This was a very amateurish job and was easy to disarm once I had traced all the circuitry. The pressure from the weight of the car would expand a small balloon placed over the end of the tube. On the skin of the balloon was a patch of metallic tape, which would touch two contacts, allowing the battery to ignite the electric blasting cap installed in the Claymore. If we had driven over that tubing, we would have been peppered with hundreds of ball bearings imbedded in the front of the Claymore.

I removed the blasting cap from the Claymore, pointed it away, and disconnected the leads from the battery. No bang, no smoke and no noise. Happy am I. Sometimes I'm lucky.

Sometimes I actually know what I'm doing. This time was a combination of both. Now the trick would be to reinstall it. I really thought Carlo's bunch had put it here but I could be mistaken. We'd be better informed tomorrow when we showed up for the meeting. I might be a little late, but I'll hear everything that goes on. We had gone to the expense of getting those phones that you can talk like it was a radio on and T.J. would have his transmit key locked down when he met Carlo tomorrow. I would be in position to hear everything and if Carlo or his boys were responsible for this, they would get it back but in a more professional setup.

As it turned out, our planning wasn't necessary. Once we got the Viper into the garage and the door closed, I decided to walk around the house and give it a good lookover. As I turned the corner by the kitchen, I could see someone lurking in the bushes by the house next door. I backed up and went around their house, hoping to sneak up on whoever it was. He must have been hard of hearing, as I'm not the quietest sneaker.

Using the shadows as best I could, I got right behind him as he was talking to someone I couldn't see. He was talking on a cell phone with one of those earpieces stuck in his ear. No wonder he didn't hear me. I waited until he finished his conversation and then chopped him on the neck with the edge of my hand. He dropped like a stone.

I carried him into the house and dropped him on the sofa. Checking though his clothes, I removed his phone and a small semi-automatic pistol he had in a shoulder holster. I got a baseball bat from the closet and sat down on the coffee table, sipping on a soda while I waited for him to wake up. T.J. sat on a stool behind the sofa and twirled a sawed-off pool cue in his fingers as he waited.

I tapped the guy on the shins with my bat figuring the pain would wake him up quicker. It did. He suddenly sat up and reached for the pistol that was no longer there. He started to jump and run when T.J. tapped him on the head lightly with his pool cue butt.

"No, no. Sit down and tell us who sent you." T.J. said.

"No habla *Ingles*." The man said, turning his head.

"Bullshit, buster. I heard you talking to someone on this phone in English." I said as I showed him the phone. "Either you talk to us or you can talk to the police with less teeth and a few broken bones. We'll say we caught you inside our house and had one of our kitchen knives in your grubby fist when we got home. Besides that, you'll have some of our expensive things in a bag with your fingerprints all over them. That constitutes armed robbery, breaking and entering and a few other things we'll dream up while you sleep from the knots on your head. That should get you fifteen to twenty years. Think about it."

His expression let us know it was sinking in when T.J. spoke up. "Time's up, buddy. Either talk or start your prayers. Makes no difference to me. You have to the count of three. One, two, ----"

"It was Fillippe's brother, Raoul. Fillippe told him if he didn't come back by seven tonight, you two would be responsible and to take you out." He quickly said.

"You build the bomb in our garage?" I asked.

"No. It was Jorge, Raoul's cousin." He said, his voice quivering.

T.J. tapped him on his head lightly and said, "On your feet. You drive here or is someone supposed to come get you?"

"My car is around the corner." He said, pointing to the east.

We went to his car together and let him get in the driver's seat and put the key in the ignition.

"Do you know what this is?" I asked as I showed him the bomb parts from our garage.

"*Si.* Yes." He said, with a scared look on his face.

I opened the back door, laid everything on the back seat except the Claymore and closed the door. He saw where I had put what he thought was a complete bomb and began shaking.

"You go straight to Jorge and have him disarm it. If the car stops more than once, even for a red light, it will go off. *Comprende?* So you'd better find a way to get to Jorge that doesn't involve traffic signals. *Vamanos.*" I said, as I slammed the back door.

T.J. and I backed up and waved him forward. He wasted no time getting away from us and left a pair of black marks on the pavement.

"How'd you set that thing up to go off if he stopped?" T.J. asked.

I pulled the Claymore out of my jacket pocket and showed it to him. He laughed so hard he had tears in his eyes. When he finally got his breath, he said, "He'll probably go crazy trying to get to Jorge without stopping or it will take him a very long time trying to miss all those lights. He's gonna be really pissed off when he gets there and finds there's no explosives. He may just come back to get even."

"What the hell, you can't live forever, now can you?" I said, as we strolled back to the house.

CHAPTER VII

"Last on the list of things to look for tonight: somebody out there is bustin' the hell out of the drug dealers. We've got six dead ones in the cooler right now, full of bullet holes and one that died from exposure and dehydration." The Sergeant said to the blue suits sitting in front of him at roll call.

"Go, somebody!" came from the back of the room.

"Now you just hold on. The scumbags that are dead have a right to respect and we have the obligation to catch and prosecute the one killing them. Murder is still against the law, the last time I looked at the book." The Sergeant said laconically. "If you happen upon whoever is murdering these drug dealers, arrest them and charge them."

"Or have a spell of hysterical blindness long enough for them to get away," came from the other side of the back of the room. The blue suits laughed and one snorted coffee through his nose on the one in front of him. A minor scuffle ensued until the Sergeant spoke again.

"In all seriousness, the only thing we know right now is that there are two of them and they are tricky. They'd have to be to put one over on these guys. Three Colombians, two Mexicans and one Jamaican full of holes and we're not sure what the other one was. It has been rumored that something big is going down this week. Charlie One-Eye told Willie Brown Shoes he overheard something down toward the wharves and Willie passed it on. Jacob, be sure to put in a voucher for the twenty you put out. Be on the lookout for two white guys riding around in a red sports car. They have short haircuts, and are about thirty or so years old. That's all Charlie heard about them, so be careful out there and come back at the end of your shift."

The men gathered up their notebooks and other gear to drift out the side door to their patrol cars. They didn't bother checking the car out, as the cars were all occupied by the previous shift coming in to fill out their reports and change to go home. The cars never rest, here.

I stepped down from the crate I was standing on below the window at the rear of the precinct house and strolled over to where T.J. was waiting in the dark gray primered Jimmy.

"They're looking for two white guys with short hair driving a red sports car for the "murder" of the drug dealers around here. We're around thirty or so, according to the Sergeant.

"It's wonderful what a case of cheap wine, fifty dollars and a knifepoint in the back will accomplish when dealing with an informant. Especially if there's a promise of another case of wine every week to come up with a different description. I doubt seriously anyone will question what Charlie One-Eye says. He's been so reliable in the past, they'll have no reason to question him in depth. Let's go see what we can get into. I've found a way to get close to the Haitians down south."

"Suits me." I replied as I got into the shotgun seat. "Where did this come from? We buy it or is it "borrowed"? I asked as T.J. sped off toward our rendezvous.

"It belonged to a little old lady that ran a nursery. She needed a truck and trailer, so I bought one and traded her for this. It's got a 454 up front and a C-6 transmission. It will go!" T.J. said with his patented 'possum grin and stuck his foot in it. One of these days, I'll learn to sit in a car with my head solidly on the head rest. That Jimmy literally leaped forward and left a trail of rubber a half block long.

"It came like this?" I asked when I got my breath back.

"Naw. I had a friend fix it up for me over the week end. It's got heavy duty suspension plus the best anti-sway bars you can buy. It tracks as good as my Viper and will keep up with it for maybe a hundred yards. We may need the speed and handling on this caper. Where we're supposed to meet them is pretty far away from anything else with only unimproved roads to drive on. Look in the back at what I've got."

I turned around carefully and my jaw dropped. T.J. must have had a hundred kilos or more all neatly stacked where the back seats used to be.

"Where'd you get all this? You rob some drug dealer already?"

"The only part of it that's the real stuff is the layer on top. The rest is fake, with just enough in it to pass the test these guys use. They're still using the old test which I figured out how to fake a long time ago. We're not selling tonight, just putting our stuff on display and setting up the trade time and place. You'll find what you need attached to the side panel."

On the side panel was a set of night vision goggles, a sawed-off shotgun with a pistol grip, and a 1911A1 model .45 caliber semi-automatic. The .45 was installed in a shoulder holster and the belt was neatly coiled in a small holder. There was also a hard sided case in a rack on the rear part of the door panel. Lifting it out of its containment, I opened it and found a breakdown sniper rifle complete with 'scope. I put the receiver and barrel together, snapped the 'scope in place and then placed the sling in its snap-on fittings.

Turning in my seat, I aimed the rifle backwards and looked through the 'scope at the receding traffic. I tried to tune down the 'scope but couldn't manage a decent picture. T.J. started laughing and I knew better, but just had to ask "What's so funny?"

"You. Trying to sight in an electronic 'scope in a moving car. That 'scope is self focusing electronically. All you have to do is sight it in on some still object and get a good picture one time and from then on, it focuses on whatever you're aiming at. It'll never work in a moving vehicle. I really should've told you before you aimed, but you know me and practical jokes. Sorry." He said as he continued to laugh.

One of these days, I'll learn not to stick my foot into T.J.'s beartraps. New year's resolution for next year: Do not trust T.J. to be rational about anything and ALWAYS check for boobytraps in everything T.J. does.

"What am I supposed to do for this caper?" I asked.

"I'm setting you up in the window of a warehouse office about sixty yards from where the "show and tell" will be going on. I'm going to let them see what I have and set up a payoff time and place for later today. You're insurance that they won't just grab and run. Besides my wearing a bulletproof vest, which I'll make sure they see, I'm going to tell them you're here watching. Just not where you are. They might try it anyway figuring to use me for a shield. Your instructions, should you choose to accept this assignment, is to make sure they don't get away."

"OK, that tells me about the sniper rifle" I said, as I broke it down and put it back in its case, "but what's all this other hardware for?"

"That comes later on in the plan. You might as well wear the pistol for insurance they didn't set up someone to take you out before the transaction starts. The possibility exists that they may have set up to take us out. I sincerely don't think they're that smart, but you know me—take out insurance before you step into the bullring."

"How long have they known where we'll meet?" I asked, as I put on the shoulder holster.

"Just three hours. That's why I don't think they'll be a problem. They may be of the impression I'm just a dumb hillbilly who lucked into a pile of stuff and am trying to make a quick buck while I can. I really don't think they'll do more than try to steal the goods outright. That's where you come in. In the event they try to take me out, you spot the head man with the laser and I believe it'll go well."

"Laser? What laser?"

"On the stock, just below the receiver, there's a thumb switch. Flick it left with your thumb and the pulsing laser will spot whatever you're aiming at. Flick it right, and it goes off. Don't use it unless I raise my hands. When I do, spot the head man dead center of his chest so's he'll see it too. If necessary, your call, put one round in the box on top of the Jimmy. The rounds in the rifle are soft noses and it will really put on a display should it be necessary."

T.J. wheeled the Jimmy inside a dilapidated warehouse and I got out along with my gear. He pointed me to the ladder I was to use to get to the office window I was to use. He had thoughtfully been there before now and laid out a trail for me to follow. I picked up the bits of paper he had used and strew them in a different manner throughout the offices to confuse anyone who might come by later. He had left a folding chair in front of the window I should use and it even had a cushion on it for my bony butt.

T.J. had taken off through the opposite door and would have circled several times before returning to the spot he had picked out for the meet. I was ready when the dealers showed up and watched two of them disappear into the shadows of the adjacent buildings. Three stayed by their SUV and waited for T. J. to show up.

It wasn't long until he did, slowly drifting down the street with his lights out, finally stopping directly in front of their SUV. He opened the door and stepped out to look all around, as if watching for cops. The three men never moved. Slowly T.J. came out from behind the door and walked toward their SUV. He stopped short, leaving five feet or so between him and them. They were talking I'm sure, but I was too far away to hear anything. Finally, T.J. turned and gestured toward the Jimmy and they all went over, ostensibly to check out T.J.'s stuff.

One of the men reached into the Jimmy and pulled out on of the bricks and stabbed a hole in it. With his knifepoint he put some of it in a small glass vial and then shook it. I couldn't see the color, but I trusted T.J. to have it turn the right color. It looked like a slow dance as they maneuvered T.J. toward a dimly lit spot in the street. T.J. maneuvered himself so that his back was to me and I got ready. I could see the two men that had gone into the shadows were now at T.J.'s back and he couldn't see them. But I could.

T.J. raised his hands slowly up to his shoulders as one of the three frisked him and turned toward the heavy man in the middle. That man laughed and reached inside his jacket just as the laser spot appeared on his chest. That stopped his laughter and he nervously began to look all around to see if he could spot me. I stopped the laser and re-sighted on the box on top of the Jimmy. A quick flick of the laser to check myself and the box literally exploded. The laser spot reappeared on the heavy man's chest and followed wherever he moved.

The heavy man turned and called to the two in the shadows. They came out of their hidden places and got in the SUV along with the other two men. T.J. and the heavy man stayed out in the open while T.J. backed up and got back into the Jimmy. He cranked it up and reversed away from the SUV for maybe fifty feet and suddenly stomped on the power. That Jimmy smoked the tires and T.J. made a moonshiners U-turn right there and disappeared in a cloud of smoke.

I watched the SUV leave and went back the way I came, taking the cushion with me. I only had to wait about ten minutes for T.J. to drift into the building and pick me up. I had already broken the sniper rifle down and as soon as I sat down, we took off, again without lights.

"Well, do we have a deal?" I asked.

"Yep. He said Carlo told him to work it this way and he had no hard feelings toward me. Just following orders."

"When do we meet for the money swap?"

"Carlo is going to call me and let me know when and where. I'll figure it from there."

The cell phone T.J. carries started to ring and he answered it. It was a short conversation and all I heard was "Uh huh and Yep". Evidently, Carlo and he were settling where and when.

After he hung up, T.J. looked thoughtful and worried as we sped down the streets. He made a fast series of turns, turned on the lights and we melted into the evening traffic. For at least twenty blocks he didn't say a word, just steered through traffic, making several around the block turns and tapping his fingers on the steering wheel. We finally pulled into on of those drive-in eateries and pulled up to the last speaker in the row. He ordered a couple of burgers with fries and two drinks, again without saying anything to me. I sure hoped half that order was mine. I was starving.

We had finished our burgers and fries and were just sipping on our drinks when T.J. cranked up the Jimmy and pulled back out into the traffic.

"Here's how it goes. We go the same place we came from and wait, just like before. You'll have to use another window to set up in and we don't have but an hour to get ready. I'll drop you off behind the building and you have to get in place without a trail to follow. Can you do it?"

"With these night vision goggles, I can. Other than the funny color, it's just like walking around in daylight. Let's do it. Same set up as before?" I asked as I readied my gear. This time I'd also take the sawed-off.

"No. If I take off my cap, put 'em all down, it's gone sour and I'm in big trouble."

This one sounded like it might be a mess, but not the worst mess we'd been in. These people were easier to deal with than the 'Cong. They couldn't disappear into a hole in the ground or the jungle. I bailed out while the Jimmy was still moving and made my way to the third floor of the warehouse where I found a chair to sit on and put my cushion on it. Easing up to the window, I saw the Jimmy arrive and park in the middle of the street. No sign of our friends yet.

I had my rifle out, the sling in place, my .45 in place in the shoulder holster and the sawed-off lying across my lap. What was real neat about this sawed-off was it was magazine fed from the bottom. Each magazine held ten rounds and I had taped two of them together upside down from the other. Push a button and the magazine dropped out, flip it over, re-insert the other magazine and "presto", another ten rounds ready to go. It was also semi-automatic. Pull the trigger and it was ready again instantly.

I settled in, ready for war. T.J. was lounging by the Jimmy on my side. He had his arms crossed over his chest and was patiently waiting for our "opponents" to show.

When they did, it was sudden and noisy. They came in shooting. T.J. dropped to the ground and rolled under the Jimmy. I sprayed their SUV with soft nose .270 rounds as fast as I could pull the trigger. Their driver was my first target, then the rear passenger with his head out the window, then the front seat passenger got his share. Their SUV crashed into the wall.

I bailed out of my seat and ran to the next window, smashing it with the butt of my rifle. Bodies were bailing out of the SUV from all portals. I got two of them, but the other three got under cover before

I could swing on them. I couldn't see T.J. but I assumed he was still under the Jimmy. The light was so bad I decided to try my night vision goggles and try that. The short period I spent putting them on gave them the chance to change places and I had to search to find them.

One was in a doorway and all I could see was his foot. Another was behind a Dumpster and I could catch glimpses of him as he bobbed up and down looking for us. The third I couldn't find at all. There is more than one way to skin a cat so I figured angles and fired a round into the door facing opposite the goon hiding there. Even soft noses will ricochet if it hits at the right angle. I heard the zing and then a whap. His body slowly slumped to the ground and his gun fell from nerveless fingers. One down—two to go.

Quickly swinging toward the one behind the Dumpster, I put two quick ones in two different places on the wall behind him. He squealed like a stuck pig and took off down the alley away from the fight. I didn't figure he'd be back, seein's he'd dropped his shooter. Now I had time to hunt for the third one. I chased every shadow I could find and he was nowhere to be found. I waited five more minutes, steadily searching, and decided to unass this spot and find another one lower down. Maybe I could spot him that way.

By the time I got set up again, I could hear sirens far off in the distance. I sure hoped they weren't looking for us, but I didn't bet against it. I tried to find T.J. and he had disappeared from under the Jimmy, but I thought I saw the shoulder of the third goober protruding from behind a wooden crate. Because it might be T.J., I decided not to pop one off and just wait. Keeping my sights on the shoulder, I could tell it was a man, but still couldn't see who it was. Damn, damn, damn.

I never was too good at waiting, so I changed views by simply moving to the next room to give myself a better angle. Now we're getting somewhere. I can see his right shoe heel, part of his calf and more of his shoulder. Rats! It's T.J.. Now what to do, what to do. T.J. decided for me by moving forward out of my sights, but the other guy still wasn't visible to me. Time to hit the street. Seeins' how I was on the street level, all I had to do was climb out the window. So I did, and got shot for my trouble. It hit me in the left arm and I dropped my rifle. Falling to my right, and rolling forward gave me the opportunity to grab my .45 and try to protect myself by rolling behind a power pole.

I wound up flat of my back and tried to shuck my night vision goggles. While I struggled with them, that damn third guy caught up to me and stood over me with a 'possum eatin' grin on his mug.

"Gotcha now, gringo. Where's the keys to the Jimmy? You tell me and I'll let you live while I take your drugs for myself."

"Man, I hurt. You shot me in the arm and I'm bleeding to death here." I moaned.

"Shut your face and tell me where the keys are." He snarled.

"In the ignition, you fool. We thought we'd have to get in and run in a hurry, so we left them in the Jimmy. Call an ambulance before you leave. I don't want to lie here and bleed to death in this dirty street."

"You're not going to bleed to death here, gringo. I'm going to shoot you in the head. You'll never know what hit you. Bye b---.

He never finished telling me bye bye because a nine millimeter round entered his forehead and exited the back of his head. He never knew what hit him.

I rolled out his falling path and got to my knees to see T.J. strolling toward me with his pistol in his hand, hanging by his side.

"Close, man. Close."

"What the hell, you're too ugly to die anyway. You'd just mess up the décor in Hades. How's your arm?"

"Pretty much normal now. Good thing Jose here didn't examine it too closely, he'd probably shot me sooner. What now, Cowboy?"

"Let's check their ride and see if they have anything of interest in it we might use." T.J. said as he ambled toward their SUV.

I finished getting up off my knees and started in the direction of their SUV to help T.J. search for whatever he thought we might use when I was struck by a blinding light and a tremendous shock wave. In the split second between the two I saw T.J. flying backward.

Arms akimbo, no hat and shirt in tatters, his body slammed through a plate glass window to my left. I dropped my goggles and shotgun to the pavement and jumped through the gaping hole T.J. had left. There were still large pieces of glass hanging in the framework, but I really didn't give a damn. T.J. had to be hurt bad and I needed to get to my only friend. Once I saw him, I damn near broke down and cried.

T.J. was flat of his back but his legs were a few feet away beyond him. He had gripped his belt with his right hand when he landed and that slowed the blood loss somewhat. His left arm I couldn't see immediately. I knelt down beside him and he stared at me through dimming eyes.

"Buddy, I can't live through this. I cut off some toes a couple of times and they wouldn't grow back, no matter how quick I stuck them on. I'm gone this time. Too much blood loss. You have to take my head so you can gain what life force I have left. Do it now before I bleed completely out! Do it!" T.J. demanded.

"I can't kill you! You're my friend!" I stammered back as I desperately looked for a way to save him.

"I can't be saved and you need the extra life force. Take that big piece of glass and cut my head off. The cops will think you tried to save me. If you don't take my head, my life force will wander until one of the others runs into it and I want you to have it. Hurry, I can feel myself slipping." He said in a slurring voice.

I picked up the largest piece of sharp glass I could find and held it above my head in line with his neck. I trembled and shook like I had a fever. I didn't think I could do this to my only friend.

T.J. smiled at me, slowly nodded his head and mouthed, "Please". I dropped the glass. It shattered and his head rolled away from his body. As it moved a blue aura emanated from it and formed small bolts of lightening on the outside. Suddenly one of the bolts grew and slammed into my body. Then another and another. They became more numerous and I could feel them getting stronger. One of them grew larger than the others and struck me in the head, jolting me so hard I fainted. Or at least I think I did. I found myself on the floor some time later staring up at the ceiling and tingling all over. I also had a monster of a headache, but as I struggled to my feet I could feel myself gaining strength.

I looked down at my friend T.J. and got another shock. His body had shriveled and his face had aged beyond belief. He looked like the oldest man in the world in his face and his body was so skinny I had a hard time recognizing him. The ring he always wore on his right hand was too big for his fingers and had fallen off. I picked it up and placed it on my right hand on the same finger T.J. had worn it on. It fit. The more I examined myself, the more I believed his story of life force leaving one body and entering another.

My arms were now as muscular as any body builder's and my legs had enlarged enough to make it hard to walk. My pants were too tight for comfort. I was now too big for my britches, no pun intended. My torso had gotten much more muscular, too. My shirt was two sizes too small, so I removed it. I felt like I had turned into the Hulk, you know, the one in comic books and on TV.

Looking down at what was left of T.J., I thought I should say goodbye in a better manner than just walking away. I knelt and said what I thought God should know about my friend and placed the remains of my shirt over his face. I needn't have bothered. His body began to smoke slightly and then just turned into a pile of ashes and dust. I looked at his head and saw another pile under my shirt. I don't think T.J. had any idea this would happen. I ran out to our Blazer and got a plastic bag, then scooped up what I could of the dust and ashes. I placed the bag in my hip pocket and got the hell out of Dodge.

Three blocks away from there, using our Blazer with no lights, I saw a drunk passed out in a stairwell. He was bigger than I used to be, so I traded him clothes. He wasn't well dressed, but at least I didn't feel strangled. I left him a fifty for the unequal trade, even though I thought he'd just spend it on booze. After that I just drove aimlessly around until I found myself at the dock where T.J. had his boat. I drove the Blazer to the other end of the pier and dumped it off the deep end. The only thing I kept was the money in bundles, the key to the boat and my bag full of T.J.

Cranking up the boat, I filled it up with gas at the marina, including the extra tanks under the forecastle or "fo'c'stle" as T.J. had called it. I had enough gas to go from here to South America if I wanted. I wanted. I figured I would hit some islands on the way and complete my journal while I thought about some things. Like, what to do now and who to do it with. I'd never really had a close friend like T.J. and would have to start over in that respect. Maybe I'd go back into the Army or the Marines. I did have good military skills and a new ID wouldn't be a problem. Something to think about. I had time, lots of time, if T.J. was any indication. He was healthy as a hog until they blew up their SUV and put him through that big glass window. Two or three years away should do the trick. By then I'd have my head on straight and will have figured out what to do with the rest of my life, however long that might be.

Longevity

Book Two

CHAPTER I

I've felt so lost since T.J. died. I drifted all over the Caribbean in my new sailboat. I sold the powerboat and bought a sailboat I could operate on my own without a crew of any kind. I fished, drank, ran the bars in the ports and still felt like a part of me was missing. Maybe it was. He had given me his blood and it still flowed in my veins, but he was no longer by my side. He was the first real friend I ever had and I missed him terribly.

So, Friday a week ago, I loaded up on provisions and decided to get away from it all by sailing to the Pacific by way of Cape Horn, through the Indian Ocean and on to Japan. I know it was a stupid idea to go so far; especially since I had only the experience of sailing in the Caribbean. But what the hell, I couldn't die so what did it matter. At least, that thought was foremost in my mind when I decided to head out. I just picked the wrong time of the year to take off. June was an especially bad time to be in that part of the Atlantic.

It was fine, the first two weeks and three days. Calm water, so to speak, and I caught plenty of fish to eat while the autopilot kept me on course. On Tuesday of the third week, during the night, the "you know what" hit the fan. The waves grew nearly as tall as my mast and that tub was rocking and rolling like a drunk at a soiree. I got the mainsail down and the foresail nearly down when the spinnaker ripped away like a leaf in a high wind. It was a high wind—a damned hurricane. I later found out it was larger than Andrew that devastated Florida in the nineties. I cranked up the diesel and tied down what I could on deck, set the auto pilot again to run with the wind and sealed myself up in the cabin to ride it out.

I took all the paperwork T.J. had left me regarding his accounts in the various banks all over the world and put them in triple sealed plastic bags, and then securely taped them to my mid section under my life jacket. If I made it through this but lost the boat, I would still have something to start over with. Providing, of course, someone found my body before the sharks made a meal of me.

Sometime after three in the morning on the second day of this fiasco, the tub rolled and I decided to get out and take my chances somewhere on top of the water instead of under it. Smartest thing I ever did while sailing. Five minutes after I got out, that worthless piece of unsinkable (according to the salesman) crap broke up and sank leaving only a few bubbles that soon dispersed in the foam of that raging sea. Me? I just lay back in my life jacket and tried to ride it out while keeping from drowning from the waves that slammed me regularly.

I have no idea how long I rode that life jacket, but it was at least a full day and a half. It had finally calmed down enough for me to doze off and when I woke it was daylight. I could see a beautiful white yacht not fifty yards from me and I started yelling and splashing like crazy. They didn't see me, I guess, because they just kept going. I remembered I had a small flare gun with five flares in a sealed bag in a pocket of my life jacket, so I unbagged it and fired it directly at the yacht. Damn, I was a good shot. It hit the rear of the pilot house and fell on the deck, still burning brightly. I could hear someone yelling, and a man came out of the pilot house, scooped it up with something and threw it overboard. I fired another, this time over the top of the yacht; didn't want to piss them off more than I already had by setting their boat on fire.

The yacht turned around and headed back in my direction, much to my relief. I was beginning to feel waterlogged, and besides, I could see shark fins breaking water in front of the yacht as it came toward me. Even knowing I couldn't die, I didn't want to test it by way of being torn to pieces. That held no glamour for me; not now, not ever. It was a pleasant surprise to find they were dolphins and not sharks. The yacht slowed down and came to a dead stop practically on top of me, lowering a rope ladder to climb up on. I grabbed the end of it and started up the side, step by step.

When I finally reached the top, the most beautiful pair of brown eyes met me with a smile underneath to match. *Damn, I have died and gone to heaven*, I thought. But it wasn't true. I climbed over the railing with a big sigh and fell flat of my back on the deck, totally exhausted. She, the angel in human form with the loveliest hair I had ever seen, knelt down and asked if I was all right. To this day I cannot tell you what she was wearing. All I could see were those gorgeous eyes, that magnificent smile and that full, lustrous head of ebon hair. I just laid there with a silly grin on my face, I'm sure.

She laughed, and I fell in love all over. I swear that laugh was like listening to angels singing and when she spoke to the man in the ice cream suit; I had no idea what she was saying. She had spoken to me in English, but this was a musical language I had no knowledge of. He turned and left us there on the deck to go wherever. I was content to just lie there and stare at her. I couldn't take my eyes off her.

That man in the ice cream suit showed up a long eternity later with a monstrous sandwich and a hot steaming cup of coffee on a tray. Someone else brought a deck chair and what looked like a TV tray to set the food on. She took my hand, helped me up with a small grunt and told me to sit and eat. Hell, I didn't want to eat; I just wanted to look at her. From nowhere, another deck chair appeared behind her and without looking, she sat down facing me. By then, she had a cup of coffee in her hand. I hadn't seen where they came from because, I suppose, I had been too busy staring at her.

"What happened?" She asked, in that marvelous voice.

"Boat sank." I replied, between bites of my sandwich, which, by the way was delicious.

She laughed again and asked how that had happened.

I told her my story, at least the part from when the storm hit me. She leaned forward and put her elbows on her knees, those exquisite knees and seemed interested in every word I said, so I kept on talking. I must have blabbed for ten minutes before she leaned back and called to someone up on deck in that language she sang so well. I had finished eating and was gulping the last of the coffee when she rose, took my hand and proceeded to lead me away. I had no idea where we were going, but I was sure it would be heavenly, wherever it might be.

She took me below deck and showed me a cabin door. "Inside you'll find a fresh set of shorts, a new shirt and some shoes. Please feel free to bathe and change. When you finish, come back up on deck and we'll talk some more; Chow" (or something that sounded like that).

The water was hot, the soap luxurious and towels soft, but I was anxious to get back to her so I hurried through the shower and quickly dressed in my new clothes. I made my way back to the deck and another man in an ice cream suit pointed to the rear of the yacht. I followed the direction of his finger and found my angel sitting facing the sea with her, oh so lovely, feet propped up on the rear rail, holding a large fishing rod. I just stood there for an eternity watching her.

She must have sensed me as she motioned for me to come to her. My pleasure entirely, I assure you. There was another canvas-seated chair beside her and I sat down, my eyes as big as saucers and slack-jawed as a teenager meeting a movie star. She glanced at me, smiled slightly and asked if I liked to fish. I hadn't done this kind before and told her so.

"Nothing to it." She said. Turning her head, she yelled up to the control deck, or somewhere behind her, said something like "oon altra" and waved those delicate fingers at her rod. Whatever reply she got did not please her at all. She turned around and glared in that direction. The man in the ice cream suit held up two fingers and disappeared somewhere to the front. Returning to face me, she said, "Good help is hard to get these days. Everyone wants a position with good pay, but doesn't want to work for it. Even though these men have been on this ship for three years, I'm going to fire Franco when we get to shore. He's gotten very snooty lately and lazier every day. My problem, not yours."

After a pause to check her rod and line, she asked me where I had been headed. I told her and then took up blabbing again. I told her, in part, about T.J. and I and left out a lot of stuff, but gave her the gist of my life. She seemed interested, even to the point of ignoring the arrival of the second rod. She nodded, smiled and I just kept on blabbing away. For some reason, I couldn't stop talking.

"Are you going to get a new boat and continue your trip when you get to shore?" she asked.

"I haven't thought that far ahead." I replied. "I definitely am going to get my money back for that "unsinkable" boat that sank.

She laughed and I heard those angels singing again. I couldn't believe I could feel like this, never having had met a woman like her in my life. I'd had girlfriends before, even contemplated marriage, but always backed away from any kind of commitment. Then the Army called and I had lost any chance I'd had with any of those women. I sure hoped this one wasn't attached and I certainly had no idea how to broach the subject.

"Where are we, exactly? Or is that a silly question?" I asked her as she again adjusted the line extending behind the boat.

"Somewhere off the coast of Spain. Not more than fifty miles, I should think. If you like, I can ask the Captain." She replied, still watching the bait dancing in the edges of the wake behind us.

I cocked my ear to the rear and began listening real hard. I thought I had heard a soft pop and felt a slight jar in the decking under my feet. I took off my shoes and turned my chair so I could see behind us. There it was again. The soft pop and the slight jar in the deck.

"How many crewmen do you have on this boat?" I asked, as I stood up and took a marlinspike from its holder and stepped to the other side to grab a gaff hook in the other hand.

"Four." She said distractedly.

Just then I saw a fog of red appear on the glass of the bridge and saw splinters of what looked like glass flying outward to the side. I grabbed her under both arms and yanked her out of her chair, dragging her backward toward the bridge. I hoped to get her out of any line of fire. I didn't make it. The crewman she had called Franco came out of the bridge's side door and fired at us. The first shot hit me in the chest and knocked me down. His second round hit her, but I couldn't see where. Franco came down the stairs and stood over her as she lay there bleeding.

"Mi dispiace, signorina. Your uncle's not going to bother my benefactor any more after I kill his only heir and when I get back, I'll kill him, too. Ciao." Franco said as he aimed the silenced pistol at her head.

He never got the shot off because I put the spike on the end of that gaff hook in his wrist and the marlinspike in his throat. Whipping the gaff hook to the left, flinging his arm away from her, I rolled hard to my left, hooked the gaff hook in his forearm and levered him overboard. I let him have the hook; they're fairly cheap.

Quickly, I checked her wound. She was bleeding profusely from her stomach. His shot had hit her abdominal aorta and she was going to bleed to death unless I could stop the bleeding. I ripped my shirt up and used it for packing, but it soaked through very rapidly. Damn, what was I going to do? I thought. Then it hit me. There was the possibility I could save her like T.J. saved me.

I ran below deck and found the medical supplies. Ripping everything apart, I found two large needles and a roll of rubber tubing and got back on deck in less than three minutes. I cut off a section of tubing to make a tourniquet for her arm and another longer piece to connect us together. I used my belt to make a tourniquet for myself.

She was already turning paler when I got the needles into her vein and mine. I sat in the deck chair in order to increase the flow from me to her. I broke out in a cold sweat when I took the packing away and she was still seeping blood. I shoved it back and stood up to get the blood flowing faster. If this didn't work, I didn't know anything else to do.

Her body suddenly jerked and that scared the bejeebers out of me. I took the packing off again for a quick look and she had stopped bleeding. As I watched, the wound began to close. Great! I thought. It's working. I removed the needle from my arm and then hers.

Her eyes opened and she moaned softly. Damned if her moaning didn't sound good. I thought sure as hell I was going to lose her out here in the middle of the ocean and no doctors anywhere. While she lay there recovering, I ran up to the bridge and slowed the engines to an idle. No point in going nowhere at speed. Back down I went and she was sitting up holding her knees and her head resting on them.

"You okay?" I queried.

"Woozy, disoriented and yet I feel stronger than I ever have. What happened? She asked.

"Franco evidently worked for someone who hates your uncle enough to kill you and he bragged he was going to kill him, too, when he got back." I replied.

Shaking her head, she asked, "Where is Franco now?"

"He went for a swim a few miles back. I don't think he'll bother us again."

"What happened to me? I swear I thought I had been shot. There's all this blood on me, but I don't hurt anywhere. Actually, I feel better than I have in years. I came out here to get away from the trees that bloom at home this time of year. I usually need to stay away for at least three weeks before my head clears up. All my congestion is gone. Besides that, I have a pretty bad skin condition that itches most of the time and I don't itch now. Did I get shot or is this Franco's blood?" She asked me.

"You got shot. Right there where the hole is in your blouse. I think your abdominal aorta got severed and I gave you a transfusion of my blood to keep you from dying."

She unbuttoned her blouse to look at the wound, which, of course, had disappeared. There was only a small pink spot on her abdomen that slowly faded as she watched. I could see her brow wrinkling and when she looked at me there was a slightly fearful look on her face.

"Oh, no. I'm not a doctor or a magician. What d'you say we head this boat for wherever we need to go to get you home and I'll tell you a story. It'll take some time to tell, so let's get this tub aimed in the right direction and I'll fix us something to eat while you play captain. Okay?"

She still looked a bit apprehensive, but took my hand and rose to my pull. We went up to the bridge to head for home. We found the

Captain lying in a pool of blood and after we had moved his body to the cooler and I had cleaned up the mess, she began the process of getting us home. I went below and did the best I could with the other two crewmen, which was put them in the cooler. After I had cleaned up most of that mess, I started a mess of my own in the tiny kitchen.

After opening every cabinet, drawer and cubbyhole, I finally found everything I needed to fix a meal for the two of us. It took me the better part of an hour to get it all done. When I got to the bridge with two plates and two glasses, she was standing there staring out the window at the setting sun behind us.

"Thanks. That looks delicious. You owe me a story and it had better be a good one. I just cut my finger on some broken glass and it healed up in less than a minute. Not only is that weird; it's impossible." She said, as she sat on a stool and began to eat, all the while looking at me as if I had antennae sticking out of my head.

"No, it's not. I'll tell you my story while we eat and maybe you'll understand everything a little better."

For the next hour, I told her almost everything, from Viet Nam to the present. I left out the particulars on how T.J. had died. Maybe after I got to know her better, I might explain about the "life force" part, but right now it really wasn't necessary. Even after I explained, she had a hard time assimilating it all. She asked questions and I answered them all as truthfully as I could. What I couldn't answer, I dodged by asking her about herself. It didn't fool her one bit, but I must say she accepted my responses.

"Am I an "Immortal" too?" she wanted to know.

"I believe so, but I'm not positive on that point. Want to try it out?"

"NO! Not right now. If the occasion arises, and it happens naturally, I'll find out soon enough. For now, let's just assume I heal quicker than I used to and leave it at that. We've got to get back to dry land and go find my uncle before something bad happens to him. Or at least warn him about Signore Verducci and his threat. OK?"

"Suits me. You do know how to run this tub, don't you?"

"Of course. I grew up on my uncle's boats and was very instrumental in the design of this particular one. I know it from stem to stern. Let's get to the bridge, uh-what did you say your name was?"

"Jason."

"Do you have a last name, Jason?"

"Believe it or not, it's Beartrack. B-e-a-r-t-r-a-c-k."

"Ooh, a Native American. That explains your lack of body hair. I wondered about that. Is it true that a Native American gets his name from the first thing his mother sees?"

"Seems like it, but I can't swear to it. Gran said it was so." I replied, as we made our way to the bridge.

She looked over the instruments, made a few changes to some of the stuff on the board and pushed the throttles forward. The boat surged forward and we were off to wherever she was taking us. I stepped outside the bridge and enjoyed the cool breeze. She joined me and I asked her who was minding the steering wheel.

"It's on autopilot for the next six hours or so; kind of like airplanes when they fly over the ocean. There's nothing in our way between here and there to worry about. It'll shut down the engines when it runs its course. I'm going to catch some shuteye before then. You should too. It's been one hell of a day, to say the least."

We went below and I crashed in my room while she slept in hers. I woke up when the engines slowed down, and knocked on her door to alert her. She didn't answer and I opened the door. She wasn't there so I went up to the bridge. She had already begun the process of piloting us to landfall. Since she seemed to know what she was doing, I went to the galley to prepare another meal for us. Chief cook and bottle washer-that's me. Not that I was complaining; she did save my hide from drowning or worse. It was the least I could do.

Once I had the meal made, I carried it up to the bridge. She was an angel to look at and a competent sailor to boot. I wondered to myself if she had other attributes I wasn't aware of.

"When we get in touch with my uncle, we don't say anything about this "Immortal" business until we get the mess with Franco straightened out. OK?"

"Sure, whatever you want. I hope you like what I fixed for you. It's all I could find in the galley."

"There's nothing in the galley I don't like. I stocked it myself before we left. Do you have any idea how this "Immortal" business works? Is it something in your genetic makeup or what?" She asked, as she fiddled with the controls.

"Beats me. All I know is after T.J. got his blood transfusion; he couldn't stay unhealed, if that makes any sense. Same with me. Now it's your turn, but I don't know if this process, whatever it is, gets diluted the further it gets away from the original. But then, I don't know who the original was or how long he or she lived. Or for that matter, if they're still alive. Your guess is as good as mine."

"Maybe Uncle Silvestro can figure it out. He's a specialist in blood borne diseases and has many friends and colleagues in the medical field that would help him."

"Let's let that ride for a while. We still need to figure out just how it's affected you and that process may prove painful. Remember the pain when you cut your finger on the glass? Fast healing and "Immortality" doesn't alleviate the pain. It's still there, just like usual. Just because you healed fast and it left no scar doesn't mean there's no pain."

"That's true, but the pain went away as fast as I healed. Have you ever 'died'? "She asked, as she ate her sandwich.

"Yes." I responded.

"What was it like while you were dead? Did you see that bright light or just darkness? Were there other people there?"

"It was very similar to having a blackout. One second you're there and the next, you're awake. Its like time passes and you aren't aware of it. Look at it this way—right now you're sitting here talking to me and then you're sitting on the floor and have no idea how long it has been or how you got there. Minus whatever pain occurred when you 'died'. That's the best I can explain it."

"Sounds to me like you don't really die, just go into a state of suspension until you heal enough to be conscious again."

"Could be. I don't know. When we get this mess with the crew and Franco out of the way, we can let Doctor Silvestro take a whack at it. Maybe he can figure it out, but I'd keep as much of this under your hat as possible. If the wrong people find out a blood transfusion from us might make them immortal, we just might wind up being nothing but blood banks."

She sat there quietly eating her sandwich and occasionally sipping her soda while looking out to sea. I could see her brow wrinkle and her eyes squint once in a while like she was trying to see something far away. Suddenly, she slapped the control panel and turned to me. "You're right. We've got to keep this a secret until we know more about how it works. Too many bad things could happen if it were common knowledge; especially to us."

"Good. Now, where are we?" I asked, as I stood up and looked out the window.

"About twenty miles from the coast of Spain. But we're not going there. We're going to Italy and dock at Brindizi, near where my Uncle Silvestro lives. He is very good friends with all the Polezei and Caribinari. At least we'll get fairer treatment from them. I don't trust the Spanish Polezei. I've had problems with them before," she added.

"How long will it take us?"

"To get to Italy? About another day and a half."

It actually took two days to get there. As we passed the coast of Spain, near the Rock of Gibraltar, we were over flown by a helicopter twice which set me a bit on edge. Just at dawn, the next day, we were approached by a fast boat with two men in the front obviously carrying weapons. I looked at them through a wonderful pair of binoculars Mila had loaned me. That's her nickname-Mila. Short for Seramila.

When I could see that the boat wasn't a police or Coast Guard vessel, I got some firepower of my own ready. She had the helm and I situated myself where it would be hard to see me from their boat. When they got within forty yards or so, they opened fire at the steering house. Mila was on the floor by then and they raked it too high to even come close to her. She had covered herself with as many life preservers as she could and wasn't even scratched, just scared silly.

Me, I lay in wait and when they got to the point of boarding, I popped up and popped them where they stood. I could see they were wearing armor, so I made nothing but head shots. Two down. How many more there were, I don't have any idea because they left in a big hurry with quite a few rounds following them. I hoped I had hit something vital when I saw smoke rise from the stern. Sure enough I had and they stopped dead in the water about a quarter mile away. We left them there and kicked our speed up southward, changing course, just in case there were others.

We boogied as fast as that thing could boogie for about three hours and zigzagged quite a bit afterward. We saw nothing but large ships the rest of the day and spent the night trading places and getting some sleep. We sailed into port the next morning about eight A.M. and put her boat in a slip near the end of the dock.

Mila called her uncle from the harbor master's phone and was told it would be about an hour before we would be picked up by her uncle's chauffeur. That left us time for breakfast at the little café across the street. A cup of cappuccino, a sweet roll and some kind of very thin pancake filled with fruit preserves kept us busy until the car showed up.

Her uncle's chauffeur parked the car and joined us for coffee, but he had espresso with grappa. Some people need a bigger eye opener than others. I'd had it before. Imagine kerosene mixed with 180 proof vodka in a small cup of coffee essence. Knock your head off and make you sweat like thoroughbred right after a race stuff. Not for me. I'd had it once at the insistence of a "friend" of mine and that was plenty.

The chauffeur finished his "eye opener" and with his head, motioned for us to get in the car. Real talkative type. Mila queried him for about four blocks, but got no verbal response, only head gestures and hand wavings. It wasn't any sign language I was familiar with, but she evidently understood him. She leaned back against my left side and snuggled up, much to my delight.

"Uncle's not in the house right now, so we have to go to his laboratory. It's going to take about thirty minutes according to Mario. So, I'll fill you in on all the sights between here and there. OK?" She said ever so sweetly.

"Suits me, but how did you understand a thing he said, or should I say "didn't say"? I never heard him make a sound." I replied.

"Mario can't talk intelligibly enough without a tongue for most people to understand, so we have worked out a silent method between us. I can understand him when he tries to talk, but that's because I've been around him since I was four. He doesn't like to talk in front of strangers. He'll get used to you after a while if you show him some patience. He may even teach you his Sicilian sign language. It's actually fairly obvious once you get the hang of it."

"I'm not going to ask how he lost his tongue; it's none of my business. I will ask him for help in communicating with him. He's not deaf, too, is he?"

"He's got better hearing than I do. Practice, I suppose. His hearing range is higher and lower than mine. I tested him once. He can hear down to sixteen cycles and up to fourteen thousand. He's just discreet about everything"

"Then he can hear me whisper in your ear "You're the cutest woman I know"? I whispered.

Mario snapped his fingers like a rifle shot and pointed at himself with a big grin.

"He thinks so, too." She said with a grin.

"Is it far to your uncle's lab, or is the time just because of the roads?" I asked.

"Mostly the roads. Some of the roads around here are the same roads the Roman army built and used. Cobblestones don't make for fast vehicle traffic. Mario knows which roads to take to give us the smoothest ride."

"I'm just worried about whoever's been after you catching us on one of these narrow little streets with no way to go but forward." I said, as I held her tighter.

"You're really a worrywart, aren't you? Take a break and give Mario some credit. He knows these roads and how to protect us from anyone or anything." She said, as she snuggled even deeper under my arm.

What the heck, I thought. The only one who can really get hurt is Mario and he certainly looks and acts capable of taking care of himself. I'm just going to enjoy the ride for as long as it lasts.

No one said anything else for fifteen minutes or so as I watched the scenery go by. It was a pleasant, calm look that I hadn't seen in a long while. I could get used to being here really well. The people I saw politely waved and went back to whatever they were doing as we traveled past them.

We started up a hill and I could see a large white building at the top as we zigzagged upward. It didn't take us long and we were in front of a modern looking building and there he was---Uncle Silvestro in the flesh. He came toward us and opened the door on Mila's side and practically yanked her out the door. They went into a whirling dance complete with cries of joy and tears were flowing down both their cheeks.

I couldn't catch it all, but he certainly was happy to see her; and her, him. They got halfway to the door and both turned at the same time and called for me to follow. At least I think that's what they said. Their gestures made up for my lack of understanding the language and I followed them inside. From the front door, it was a short walk to a set of elevators which we boarded. They were still yammering away in Italian when she punched a button on the wall and the door closed. I still find it hard to tell if I'm going up or down without looking at the numbers flash by.

We were going down, but how far I couldn't tell. There weren't any numbers. I had nothing better to do anyway, so I eavesdropped. I could catch about every third or fourth word, and realized she was telling him about me, the rat that shot her and the other jerks that tried again in the Mediterranean. He didn't seem to be shocked, just concerned.

Turning to me, he asked, "Were they after you or her?"

"Her, I'm sure. My boat had sunk and no one knew where I was anyway. I didn't file a sailing plan; I just took off after my best friend died. The one that killed her crew mentioned you by name, or at least your relationship to her. I really don't remember the exact words." I replied.

"He's right. I remember him saying "your Uncle" and something about his benefactor, Signore Verducci, just before he was going to shoot me again."

"What? He shot you? Where? Are you alright? Let me see; maybe I can help." Silvestro exclaimed.

That's about when the doors opened and we got off the elevator. I glanced at the sign next to the door and it said SEI-B. I asked what the sign said and Mila said "Six-Bee. B is for basement."

Silvestro was still rattling away in Italian and Mila told him to speak English until I could learn enough to follow in Italian.

"What do you mean you got shot? How badly were you hurt? You couldn't have been hurt badly, you seem fine now. Show me where you got shot." Silvestro almost shouted.

"When we get into the lab and the doors are locked, I'll explain the whole thing from beginning to end, OK?"

That seemed to pacify him, but didn't slow him down one bit. We hurried down a corridor, turned two or three corners and got in another elevator. We went down some more, but this time it had numbers and I watched as we dropped six more levels. When it stopped, this time we went out the back of the elevator instead of the front. Really weird place, this lab of Silvestro's.

Down we went another long corridor to a door that looked like a bank vault. Silvestro entered some numbers on a pad beside the door and then placed his hand on a glass plate below it. The door clicked loudly and opened into a small anteroom. When he shut the door, we were bathed in a bright blue light and some huge fan blew the air in every direction. Damn, Mila has some great legs, too.

When everything had stopped and the blue light had gone off, the next door opened and we were in one of the largest laboratories I had ever seen. They ignored everything and headed to the right toward a regular door with Silvestro's name and title on it. Upon entering, Silvestro locked it with a key.

"Now, what's the big secret about you getting shot?" He demanded, with his fists on his hips.

"I died" Mila stated flatly.

Silvestro started off in loud Italian again and Mila reminded him to speak English.

"Not possible. You are here, alive and well. You could not have "died" and still be here unless your friend, Jason here, is a miracle man. Are you a miracle man, Jason Beartrack? Or are you some kind of hypnotist who has made Mila believe she died?"

"Uncle, sit down and I'll show you something that will amaze you. Sit!"

He sat.

She went over to the small lab set up in the corner and returned with a small scalpel. She then picked up Silvestro's hand and scratched him lightly on his forearm with the blade. He said nothing, but continued to watch the scalpel in her hand. She placed the scalpel in the web between her left thumb and forefinger with the blade facing up, shoved it in and ripped it upward. The blood flew and Silvestro's eyes grew big, but he said nothing as he yanked a handkerchief from his coat pocket and tried to stem the flow of blood from her hand. She jerked away and blocked him from touching the wound.

The blood flow stopped as he watched with goggle-eyed wonder and the skin grew back together right there in front of him. She held her hand out for him to hold as he watched the wound turn from bright pink back to her normal skin color, a most beautiful olive.

The line where she had cut herself diminished to nothing and faded away. He couldn't believe what he had seen. He turned her hand over several times looking for some sign of damage and couldn't find any. Me? I just sat there and kept my mouth shut.

Silvestro literally fell into his chair and sat there slack-jawed at what he had seen.

"Uncle, I don't want to demonstrate this again. It hurt like the dickens, but as you can see, I healed very rapidly. Stay where you are and I and Jason will tell you a story. Once we're through, you may speak, but not before then," she stated as she pulled up a comfortable chair and began at the point where she had picked me out of the sea.

Most of the time she spoke in English, but occasionally she reverted to Italian. It took quite a while for her to get through it all, but I must admire Silvestro in his ability not to interrupt her. He began listening with incredulity, changing to horror when the part about her dying came forth and finally to pensiveness as the tale wound down to our docking. When she stopped, he just sat there thinking and absorbing it all. Then it was my turn.

I started with my getting wounded in Viet Nam and as my story unraveled, Silvestro paid close attention. I could see his mind working furiously behind his facial expressions, but again he did not interrupt my tale. It looked like he experienced physical pain when I told him how T.J. had died. Then the same face appeared when I told him about Mila getting shot on the boat. When I had finished, he slowly rose and said, "I think I need a stiff drink." Hell, we all had one with him. Nothing more was said for about ten minutes.

"I think I need to examine some of your blood, both of you, and try to see if there is a significant difference in your blood as opposed to mine. I don't think blood type has anything to do with this phenomenon, but there must be something we can see through a microscope. If we can isolate it----think of the possibilities," Silvestro mused.

"That's what scares the both of us." Mila said with a trembling voice. "If you can discover what it is that does this, and cannot duplicate it, it will create chaos. We'd become nothing more than blood banks and no longer be able to be us—just donors. If you can duplicate it, how can this world survive if everyone becomes immortal? We **and** you must be very careful, Uncle."

Silvestro looked startled. Then as he thought about it for a while, he began nodding his head and mumbling to himself. Finally, after pacing for quite a while, he stopped and said, "You're right. We must keep a tight rein on our research and not allow others to work on this."

I stuck my two cents worth in then and said, "I would much prefer that scenario. Like Mila says, we'd become prisoners of whomever could trap and hold us. I don't want to live like that and I'm sure you'd not like Mila to become just someone's source of blood to make them live longer. At this point, I know Mila heals as swiftly as I do, but I can't be sure she can pass it on. I know I can simply because of Mila. That's one of the things we need to know—how far down the line can it go or am I the last link in this chain?"

Mila looked surprised at what I had said, then after a moment's thought she agreed with me. "Uncle, he's right. We don't know and we need to find out without anyone else discovering our secret. Do you think there's a way to find out?"

"Of course, my dear Mila. There's surely a method of extracting that information from your blood and Jason's. We'll start on it first thing in the morning. The most important thing right now is a good meal and a night's rest. I'm worn out and I'm sure you two are also. Allora, a casa per china e' un bona notte a letto. Andiamo." he said with exuberance as he headed for the door.

CHAPTER II

Silvestro had a cook who really knew her stuff. I couldn't stop eating and drinking the excellent wine she served. I ate so much I could hardly waddle away from the table to the salon where she served dessert. A Tiramisu that literally melted in your mouth. I only had a small piece because I was so stuffed I could hardly move. Mila and Silvestro were talking a mile a minute in Italian and since I couldn't catch much of it, I dozed off in a very comfortable chair.

I awoke around two a.m. and found myself covered with a soft blanket, obviously hand made and older than I. There was a small light on and I could see a note by my chair that read–"You looked so comfortable I couldn't bear to wake you. Your room is directly ahead of you, two doors down on the right. See you in the morning. Mila." It felt so nice there in the chair, I just re-covered myself and went back to sleep.

I awoke again about five thirty and went looking for a *bagno.* I first went to what had been identified as my room to see if there was a private bathroom. Nope. So I continued my search and there it was dead center at the end of the hall. Nicely done with terrazzo floors and marble accouterments throughout. After washing up, I went hunting for the kitchen where I found Mario at a small table, drinking his espresso with grappa. Motioning for me to sit, he got a regular size mug and poured a cup of steaming coffee for me. I tasted it and found he did know how to make good coffee. I put half a teaspoon of sugar in the cup and settled in to learn Mario's sign language. He had a small tablet with a pencil and could write English very well. He would sign something, write it down and sign it again. Smart boy that I am, within an hour I could carry on a passable conversation with him. To be really truthful, I spoke "baby talk" in his sign language, but he understood anyway. I think if I hang around him long enough, I might get proficient.

We were so busy yakking, I didn't hear anyone enter the kitchen, but Mario got up again and poured another cup of coffee. It was then I heard Mila's shuffling steps as she entered the room. She had combed her hair, but hadn't bothered with make-up. God, she was gorgeous in the morning light. She still had one eye closed when she started in on the coffee and refused to even say "Good Morning" until she was half way through the coffee in her cup.

"I'm a beast until I've had my coffee. I'm sorry, but Mario knows how grouchy I am when I first wake up. That's why he gets up first and has coffee ready when I drag into the kitchen."

"Then we are complementary. When I get tired and sleepy late in the day, I either go to sleep or get surly. I like mornings much better because I'm usually rested. We make a nice pair."

Raising one eyebrow, she thought about that, and then smiled.

"I think today we may find out just how nice a pair we are. Uncle Silvestro is going to take a blood sample from each of us and one from himself and compare them in his lab. This should really be interesting." she said over the rim of her coffee cup.

Silvestro's voice boomed down the hallway, "You two come on. We don't have all day. I need to get started on this as soon as possible."

"Duty calls and the vampire awaits," I said jokingly.

Mila smiled again, picked up her cup and we ambled and shuffled down the hallway to Silvestro's office. Once there, he took blood samples from both of us and Mila took his. Waving us off like children, he immediately went to work. Not having any idea of what was going on, I wandered off to explore. Mario met me in the hall and motioned me to follow.

He opened doors, pointed at things and through our sign language I got the gist of his narrative. Big place-lots of rooms, equipment and more people than I could count. Mario "told" me about the research going on here, which was mostly pharmaceutical in nature.

Silvestro's company was monetarily huge, but this complex was his only one. When Mario showed me the blueprints for the complex, I was surprised at how much of it was underground and Silvestro's expansion plans were for more underground wings to be built.

"How is that done?" I asked.

Mario "told" me about the other branch of the family that were primarily quarriers and miners that did all his work for him. All the debris from the excavations was disposed of in their abandoned quarries except for whatever good stone they removed. Much of the good stone was sold to offset the cost of transportation of the junk and the rest they used in their own business. All in all, profitable for them both. Silvestro got a good price on the excavation and the quarriers made money on the excavated material.

As we made our way back to the lab, Mario stopped and appeared to be listening intently. He held up a hand to quiet me and we crept silently down one of the newly excavated side tunnels. When we got to the end of it, even I could hear a muffled banging noise. Rushing back to the head of the tunnel, leaving me standing near the wall, Mario opened a locker just inside the complex. He brought back what appeared to be some sort of equipment case. It turned out to be a very sophisticated listening device which he used to locate the direction the noise was coming from. The machine indicated it was coming from the face of the tunnel and was originating from a distance of between forty and fifty feet away.

Closing up the case, Mario indicated we should leave. He put away the case and we rushed upstairs to Silvestro's lab to let him know what we had found. Silvestro picked up his phone and called what I thought might be security. Satisfied, Silvestro explained that his family was working on another leg of the tunnels and their work appeared to be what we had heard. Mario doubted this and went to check it out for himself.

Silvestro went back to his work on the blood samples he had taken. I figured I should follow Mario in case he needed help. I left Silvestro's lab and made my way to where Mario was accumulating his gear. His gear included two shotguns and the listening machine. We went to the elevator and I followed him into another section that we had not visited. When we got to a large metal door that looked like it belonged on a battleship, Mario attached the listening thing to the wall and patiently waited for it to warm up and tell him something. He grinned and pointed to the door. This must be the section the noise was coming from. Mario unslung one of the shotguns and handed it to me. After checking the load, I stood back and pointed it at the door. Mario opened it and then we stepped through. The noise was evidently farther down the tunnel. Lights were strung along the ceiling on wires attached to hooks driven into the bare rock. The tunnel turned sharply to the left about forty yards away and we couldn't see what was making the noise.

Mario latched the door and we proceeded toward the turn in the tunnel. Swiftly, on soft- soled shoes that didn't make any noise, we arrived at the bend in the tunnel. Holding up one hand to stop me, Mario took out of his pocket a small mirror on an extendable rod, holding it close to the floor; he used it to see around the corner. He held up three fingers and waggled his hand as if to tell me something, but this I didn't understand. He motioned for me to advance to the opposite side of the tunnel and stand guard.

Bringing his shotgun to a ready position, he went around the corner and disappeared from my view. I couldn't let him face danger by himself, so I stepped across the tunnel to the far side and brought my shotgun up to my shoulder, ready to fire. Mario had already slung his shotgun over his shoulder again and was talking to three men. The noise had stopped as they had laid down their tools. They evidently hadn't seen me so far, and were animatedly conversing with Mario in his sign language. He didn't appear upset, so I advanced toward them. One of the three men moved over to Mario's left side and then slightly behind him. As he did so, I could see he had a pistol stuck in his belt at the back.

As he sidled behind Mario, he reached behind himself and began to draw the pistol out. The other two men and Mario were ostensibly discussing how the tunnel should be dug and were not looking toward me. As the one man drew the pistol, his arm ran into the barrel of my shotgun, which I had placed near his right kidney. His back stiffened, and he gasped. Mario unslung his shotgun in an instant, stepped to his right and had the other two covered so fast they had no chance to reach for any weapon they might have.

"On your knees." I said to the one I had covered with my shotgun.

He slowly sank down and let go of the pistol as he raised his hands. The other two followed suit. I stepped back far enough to cover them all as Mario searched them for weapons, all the while holding his shotgun against their bodies. Mario found that all three had pistols hidden on their bodies. He searched their tools and gear, finding dynamite, blasting caps and two sub-machine guns.

They had more dynamite than was needed to enlarge the drift they were working on. Further searching by Mario, as I closely guarded the three men, revealed they were using a large canvas to hide a different drift that would lead to the back of the largest lab area in Silvestro's complex. Yanking the canvas from the wall, Mario paced the distance down the drift and made notes on a small pad. When he returned, we trussed up the three men and returned to the main entrance to this tunnel. He unlatched the door and I stepped inside to guard them as they came through.

Once inside, Mario again latched the door and flipped a switch to return the air pressure in the drift to less than the complex. Not a vacuum, just enough negative pressure to keep dust out of the complex. We started back to the elevators and about half way down the tunnel, the last man stumbled, knocking the next one down who knocked the third one into me. I fell to one knee and the first man attempted to kick Mario. Mario was too swift and the kick missed. I wasn't so lucky. The first man in line had rolled over and I got a boot straight into my jaw. The force of that put my head hard against the wall and the lights went out.

I woke up with my head in Mila's lap and a cool compress on my jaw. Except for a throbbing head and a sore jaw, I wasn't hurt. I couldn't say as much for the three men we had captured. Two were dead and the other wasn't in very good health. Mario hadn't done a very good job of searching them for weapons. They all had knives and had tried to use them against Mario. Mario told me later that he feared to fire his shotgun because I was in the midst of the three men and he was afraid he'd hit me. He had kicked the last man in line so hard under his chin that it had snapped his neck. He'd taken away the knife from the man that had kicked me and returned it to him, point first. The middle man was lucky, so to speak. Mario had popped him across the head with the butt of his shotgun and had only broken his jaw and torn his ear up badly.

The Caribinari were already there and had finished their investigation by the time I was able to get off the floor. I was still pretty dizzy and Silvestro advised me to go lie down and take it easy for a couple of hours. As Mila held onto me, we went back upstairs and I lay down on a couch. The dizziness had long since passed, but I was enjoying being close to Mila so much, I kept my mouth shut and let her help me. She got another cold cloth and soothed my brow again. I sighed, and she leaned over to kiss my brow. I reached up and pulled her lips to mine.

Before my lips touched hers, Mila whispered, "Are you very sure this is what you want to do?" My only response was to kiss her gently and hold her head softly. My fingers were entwined in her lovely hair and she didn't pull back. If she had, I would have let go instantly. She moaned softly and placed her hands on the side of my face with a touch as light as the landing of a butterfly. I opened my eyes and found her staring at me. She then closed her eyes, took a short breath and returned the kiss like I had never been kissed before. I damn near fainted.

After an eternity of bliss, she slowly backed away and I let her go, following her with my eyes. She folded her hands on her lap and just sat there. I took her hands in mine and let her alone. I had no idea what to say or do. She looked as if she was in pain and she was silently crying; big teardrops running down her face and splashing onto our hands.

"There's something you have to know . . .," she started, but didn't finish as I placed my hand over her mouth.

"Whatever it is, I don't need to know now. When you know me better– maybe. But not now. We've only just begun and we both need to know the other better before we confess our various sins, mistakes, etc., don't you think?"

With a large smile across her face, she wiped the tears away and replied, "No. I need to tell you this now, not later. So shut up, lay back and listen."

I shut up, lay back, and listened.

"When we picked you up out in the sea, I thought I had found the most gorgeous thing I had ever seen in my life. Once you cleaned up, I knew I had. All this time I have been hiding my feelings as best I could. I thought you had no feelings for me and I didn't want to force anything. It is not proper for a woman to advance toward a man, and I had a very difficult time hiding what I felt for you. Besides being very, very handsome, you have a good heart and are courageous. The more I was around you, the more I wanted to tell you my feelings, but couldn't. I cried just then because I knew, deep in my heart, that what you feel for me isn't just a physical attraction, but love. Am I right?" She asked, again with that worried look on her wonderful face.

I yelled, jumped up from the couch, grabbed her and spun her around. "I knew you were smarter than me; I just didn't know until now just how much smarter you are. Yes, Yes, Yes, I love you. As soon as I saw your face and heard that voice, I knew you were the one for me, but I didn't know how to tell you. I thought of every way possible, but couldn't think of a way. And I was afraid of your Uncle Silvestro."

"There's no reason to be afraid of Uncle Silvestro. He's as gentle as a lamb."

"I know that now, but Mario's big and spooky enough and your uncle isn't a small man. Between the two of them, I was afraid if I made them mad, there'd be trouble."

"You are a silly goose and I love you for it. Let's tell Uncle Silvestro. I'll bet he'll be happy for us."

"Tell him what?"

"That we're going to get married, of course."

"I don't remember asking, but let me remedy that right now." I said, as I knelt on one knee in front of her. "My lovely Seramila, will you take this beat up, ugly American for your husband? I love you and want you to be my wife until death do us part."

"If we're both immortal, that'll be a very long time. Are you sure that's what you want?" Mila responded.

"I'm more than willing if you are. Will you marry me?" I asked again, as I kissed her hand.

"Yes, yes, yes. Until death do us part. Now get up and kiss me again. I like the way you do that."

Being of sound mind, I promptly followed her instructions until Silvestro came booming into the room some time later. Who know how long it was, I certainly wasn't keeping track of time.

"Will you two stop that! I need more blood samples if I'm ever going to determine what you two have in your blood besides romance. When do I have to pay for the wedding, Mila?"

"Who said we're getting married, Uncle?"

"I may be old, but I'm not stupid. I eavesdropped before I came in. Welcome to the family, Jason. I hope you survive the ordeal. Now come along and give me some more blood, the both of you!" he bellowed as he turned and headed back to his lab.

We followed him back to the lab and gave him two vials of blood each. He took two from himself and two from Mario as well. Waving us away with the back of his hand, he turned back to his microscope and began his work. He wasn't ignoring us, just engrossed in his work. Mila told me later he has always been that way — once he gets an idea in his head, he doesn't stop until he either figures it out or decides that an answer is impossible.

Mario drove us into the nearby village where he introduced us to a family member of his that was a broker for a jewelry business. His cousin (I think) was currently on vacation but assured us he could get his hands on some fine engagement rings for Mila to look over. If none of them suited her, he would take us to Rome on the train and visit a few of his dealers.

He assured me he could get whatever Mila wanted at "a good price." Money was no object to me, but I didn't tell him that. If there is one thing Italians like to do, it's haggle over prices. I had no intention of telling him I was wealthy. Mila didn't even know that at this point. It would be a wedding surprise from me, but after the wedding.

When we got back to the lab, Silvestro was very excited about something he was looking at through his microscope.

"Come here and look at this Mila. You too, Jason I think I've found what is different about your blood."

As we each looked, he explained what to look for and even dumb old me could see the difference. His red blood cells were round in shape and had a depression in the center on both sides. Ours were round in shape, but were like doughnuts — they had a hole in the center. When he magnified them further, they appeared to have filaments connecting from one side to the other. Sort of like those dream-catchers the American Indians made. The filaments weren't in a random pattern, but I couldn't see just what kind of pattern it made until Mila pointed it out to me.

"It looks like a seven pointed star with a hexagon in the middle. Look closely and you can see the pattern."

I focused the 'scope a bit and then it jumped out at me. There it was— the seven pointed star with that hexagon shape in the middle of the donut hole.

"What does that tell you, Silvestro?" I asked, as I rose up from the eyepiece of the microscope.

"How should I know? I just found the difference this morning. It is a large difference, but what significance it has, I have absolutely no idea. I have many more hours of research before me, but even then I may not ever learn why it is different. I suspect some things, but I shall keep them to myself until learn more. Besides, my suspicions may be all wet. Who knows? Now get out of here and go play lovey-dovey somewhere and let me get back to work." Silvestro ordered, as he waved us away with his characteristic back of his hand wave.

Since Mila and I could not do whatever Silvestro did in his lab, we decided to go swimming at the nice little beach over the hill. Mario would bodyguard/chaperone us.

CHAPTER III

Mario loaded up half the kitchen, it seemed, for just an afternoon at the beach. He brought along enough food for what seemed a small army could eat. Mila didn't object at all, so neither did I. Mario drove, Mila and I sat up front with him and the food occupied most of the back seat. It was only a fifteen minute walk to the beach, but it took us forty five minutes in the car. I would have sworn we went in two or three circles before we got there, but didn't bother commenting. Mario had his ways, and nothing would change them, not even Silvestro.

We got the blankets, towels and assorted creams, lotions and such out of the car. Mario took care of the rest. He frowned when I started to help him - 'nuff said. I let him have his way and Mila just smiled, then headed down the hill to the beach. Smart me - I followed Mila and left Mario to his chores. Much more delightful following Mila downhill to the beach.

After spreading out the beach blankets on the beautiful white sand, Mila made herself comfortable and began lathering lotion all over herself. I quickly volunteered my services and she handed me the lotion with a smile. She gathered her hair up into a rough bun and pinned it in place on top of her head while I spread lotion where it was needed.

When I finished lotioning her, she turned, took the bottle from me, and began to apply lotion to my exposed skin. I had never had that done to me before and it was both sensual and soothing at the same time. I almost went to sleep, it was so calming.

When Mila had me all lotioned up, she took off for the water and dove right in, head first. I followed suit. I had thought the water would be cool, at least. It felt almost as warm as a bath in your own home. Opening my eyes, I followed her downward and we passed through a layer of cooler water and back up into the warm water. The thermocline seemed to be about ten or fifteen feet down, not too deep to free dive.

We porpoised in and out of the cool water and in and out of the air. Breathe, dive through warm into cool, back into warm and up to breathe once again. It was a lot of fun, but tiring. I signaled Mila to head for the beach and we turned shoreward. Between us and the shore was a fin. A large fin. It wasn't a dolphin fin. It was a shark fin. We faced it and trod water together.

We circled and the shark circled, but came no closer. It seemed to be alone and lone sharks, except for great whites and tigers, are basically cowards. Most sharks prefer to hunt in packs. This one was fairly large and alone. We tried to edge closer to shore as we trod water and was pretty successful for a while. When we got about thirty yards, the shark began circling faster, making it harder to keep up with him.

Mila began whistling. It wasn't a tune, more like a signal in Morse code combined with bird calls. I caught a glimpse of Mario racing toward the car, but got distracted when the shark fin disappeared. I ducked my head under water to check on him and saw it going away from us. I told Mila and she said keep an eye on it, it might be preparing for an attack run. Back under water went my head and sure enough, it was returning at a higher rate of speed. When it got close, I yelled underwater. The shark turned sharply and started making large circles again.

Mario walked into the water to about waist deep, which put him about twenty five yards away from us. The shark was circling us at about fifteen yards. When the shark was nearest Mario, he tossed a baseball sized object underhanded in front of the shark. It arced about ten feet high and hit the water four or five feet in front of the shark. The shark then leaped out of the water along with a lot of water and seaweed. As it sailed through the air, I could see it was bleeding and in more than one piece. Damned if Mario hadn't hit under it with a grenade and kept us from being shark lunch. Hell'uv'a good underhand toss. Great timing, too!

We got out of the water as fast as we could swim, while Mario collected pieces of the shark that had landed on the beach, which was most of it. It had been a tiger shark, one of the few man-eaters. The strange thing was no sharks had ever been sighted at or near this stretch of beach. Silvestro had installed a very good shark net years ago and as far as Mila knew, the maintenance had been kept up. We needed to check this out and soon because the local villagers use this beach, too.

Mila, Mario and I pulled the remains of the tiger shark up beyond the high tide mark and headed back to get a truck to load the thing up in. As soon as we got back, Silvestro came out and demanded to know what had caused the explosion he had heard. He knew Mario carried many weapons and other devices as part of his duties as bodyguard. Excitement reigned supreme for a few minutes until we explained the whole story. Silvestro finally calmed down.

"Mario, you're going to be the death of me. I never know if you're protecting Mila or someone has gotten past your guard and gotten the both of you. I'm going to have to figure out a way to communicate with you at a distance. Have you any suggestions?" Silvestro asked.

Mario just shrugged and went about the business of getting what he needed together to recover the tiger shark. Nothing seemed to fluster Mario. Mila suggested she and I carry cell phones from now on in order to ease Silvestro's mind. He agreed and immediately yelled at another of his assistants who scurried off into the labyrinth of the laboratory.

"Pietro will either get two of the labs cells for you two to carry or will obtain two new ones before the end of the day. As soon as you get through with the shark, come to my lab. We need to talk." Silvestro stated, wagging his finger at the both of us.

Mila smiled, wiggled her fingers at Silvestro as he turned and left, and then took my elbow to lead me over to the truck. I knew where the truck was, but I let her lead me anyway. You know me; anything to stay near Mila. No way around it. I was as love struck as a teenager.

We walked hand in hand to the beach and left Mario to get all the gear together. As we walked, I was thinking about how the shark could have gotten past the shark nets. I decided after we recovered the shark and went to see what Silvestro wanted, I would take a boat out to the nets and see what I could see. Scuba gear was no problem as Silvestro had plenty at his disposal. I thought about taking Mario with me in the boat, just in case.

"After we collect the shark remains and see what Uncle Silvestro wants with us in his lab, I think you; Mario and I should get some scuba gear and check out the nets." Mila said just as we reached the sands of the beach.

Startled, I blurted out, "That's exactly what I was thinking of doing. Do our minds run on the same track or can you read minds now?"

Puzzled, Mila thought a minute and shrugged. "I don't know, but it seemed like the thought just jumped into my mind a few seconds ago. We probably think a lot alike, both of us being of the same blood now."

"Now you've got me intrigued. T.J. and I seemed to think of the same things at the same time and when we worked together, it was like we didn't need to talk, we just did what was needed at the same time or in the order needed. Wonder how we could check that out?"

"After we see what Uncle Silvestro wants of us in the lab, we'll ask him if he knows of a way to check that out. If he doesn't, I'll bet he knows someone who would know. His network of scientific friends spans the globe, even into Russia."

"Okay, but I really do want to check this out"

Just then, Mario showed up with a flatbed truck with dual rear wheels. Up near the cab were a winch and a small a-frame. It looked sturdy enough to pull what was left of the tiger shark up onto the bed. When he stopped, I could see ramp boards stacked in racks on the side of the truck. Whoever owned this truck came prepared for almost anything.

Mario backed up the truck to the edge of the sandy beach and I took the ramp planks from their racks. Placing them at the rear of the truck bed, I dropped the tabs on the planks into the slots provided. We now had a ramp as wide as the truck. Mario fired up the pony engine for the winch, started playing out cable, while Mila took chains out of storage boxes underneath the truck bed.

Mario put on some long sleeved gloves, placed the chains around the largest pieces of the tiger shark and Mila operated the controls of the winch. It went a lot faster than I had expected and we had finished up in half an hour. Mario threw a tarp over the carcass and made signs to Mila. Mila signed back and Mario left without further ado.

"Mario is taking the shark to the port to a friend of his. His friend will take care of the remains. The meat and cartilage will probably end up as cat food before the day has ended." Mila commented as she again took my hand in hers.

"Cat food sounds good to me. I've tried shark, but ever since I found out they have no kidneys and dispose of their waste water through their skin, I've sort of lost my taste for shark."

"I've never tried it and am not going to." Mila stated emphatically. "I cannot even eat calamari after watching the creatures on the Discovery Channel. They are just too intelligent for me to eat.

Americans have an aversion to horsemeat solely based on emotions and I can base my tastes on emotions, too!"

"Never let it be said I disagreed with you on that subject. I've eaten some strange things that other people won't eat that tastes good to me. Then again, no matter how hard I tried, I couldn't eat the fried rice bugs Southeast Asians consider a delicacy. Looks too much like a roach to me."

We strolled back up the beach and over the small hills to Silvestro's lab to see what it was he wanted. Once inside his office, we found him poring over some typed pages and alternately looking through his microscope and then back at the pages. Not wanting to interrupt him at his work, we sat down and watched. He seemed oblivious to our presence for the better part of fifteen minutes.

"You two need to look at what else we've found out about that funny blood of yours. Hector tried to destroy part of a blood sample by searing it with a laser beam and as soon as he stopped the beam, the blood returned to normal and all the damaged parts became undamaged. This happened in a Petri dish! How can a blood sample, outside a human body, react in this manner? It seemed to be impossible, but I tried it myself and came up with the same results. Another thing: we killed a mouse by extracting all the oxygen out of his habitat and within one minute of injecting only one half cc of Mila's blood into him, the mouse came back to life. In less than ten minutes he was eating and going after one of the females. I cannot believe what I have seen with my own eyes! What do you think of that?" Silvestro excitedly exclaimed, all the while going round and around his desk, waving his arms like a maestro directing a fast piece of music.

Mila and I looked at each other and shrugged at the same time. "I have absolutely no idea what is going on or what is possible, Uncle Silvestro. I brought Jason here because I thought you might be able to tell us about this strangeness we both endure. If you are stumped, we are more so."

"Stumped? Who said I was stumped? It was a rhetorical question anyway. I was only thinking out loud. It was more for your information and to keep you up to date than anything else. Go play lovey-dovey somewhere and let me get back to work. I have many more tests to run before I am stumped. By the way, we removed some blood from that first mouse and put it in another mouse and tried to kill it the same way. Three times it has revived itself this afternoon and is now running a maze test the other mouse learned last week. I'll let you know those results tomorrow. Now go away."

We went away. Mario was back and putting things away when we got to the tool building. Most people say "tool shed". This "tool shed" was big enough to hold a Lear jet and then some. He had enough tools and equipment in this building to keep a brigade busy for a week, just inventorying everything that didn't pertain to the jet plane at the far end.

"Do we look at the nets today or wait until tomorrow?" Mila asked.

After consulting my watch and seeing that it was after five PM, I replied that we should wait until we had enough light to explore the full length of the net, not just part of it.

"Then let's go get something to eat and plan out tomorrow – or whatever." Mila said.

I especially liked the "whatever" but would settle for something to eat as long as it wasn't too heavy. A nice salad, some pasta and a little dessert would suit me fine. Mila led off in the direction of the near-by village where she said was a nice little cafe´ run by an old couple she claimed really knew how to cook. By the time we got there, I was hungry enough to eat a horse. The path Mila took to get us to the cafe´ would have suited a Marine Drill Sergeant. My feet hurt all the way up to my eyebrows.

Mila ordered some wine and an appetizer for us while we waited for our order to be prepared. She ordered it and I had no idea what it might be. She spoke to them in an Italian dialect I had no knowledge of. I only caught two words –fresca and bene. She had never steered me wrong before so I didn't ask. I learned long ago to eat it today and ask what it was tomorrow. That way, your stomach won't rebel in front of friends.

The appetizer was good, the wine was excellent – a homemade red – and the salad they presented was totally fresh. It even came with a live ladybug, which I let go outside. We talked about everything and nothing. We passed up talking about today's events and just enjoyed each other's company. The main course came and it turned us into mutes. It tasted so good we had no time for talking. The proprietress, Nona, came out occasionally to check on things, but Mila waved her off each time. I saw the old man but once. I found out later he was in the kitchen, but was only watching television. That's one thing I liked about Italian television: the programs run uninterrupted from start to finish and all the commercials come after the program is completed.

After the meal, Mila and I sipped some more of that excellent wine and talked a while longer. Nona brought us a tiramisu that melted in our mouths and then a small orange sorbet, followed by cappucino with shredded dark chocolate on top of the foam. Absolutely decadent.

By the time we had had enough, I looked at my watch and it was a quarter of eleven. I dreaded the walk back, but Mila had other ideas. I really enjoyed the carriage ride.

Silvestro was a nice guy, but I knew Mila and I had to go our separate ways once we went inside. Sure enough Silvestro was still up, but once Mila had said goodnight, he trundled off to bed himself. I took a shower and shaved, changed into my sleeping outfit – shorts and a t-shirt– and lay down on my bed only to stare at the ceiling for the better part of an hour. I know how long it was because I could see the clock on my dresser staring at me with its green numbers for eyes.

I tried several different positions to try to get to sleep, but was failing miserably. Perhaps it was the cappucino, but it had never bothered me before now. For another fifteen minutes I tried to sleep, but it still escaped me, so I got up and put on my pants and some sandals. Maybe a little walk in the fresh air would relax me enough to get to sleep.

I stepped outside and stood still for a while as my eyes adjusted to the moonlight. I didn't want to trip over anything. To my right, about forty yards away, was a little gazebo covered in grapevines that I remembered from this afternoon. It looked inviting, so I carefully made my way over toward the bench I remembered was in the middle. It wasn't there any more.

In the leaf dappled shadows I could see a light colored square lying on the floor of the gazebo. Upon closer examination, I found it was an air mattress complete with pillows, sheets, a light blanket and Mila.

"I was beginning to think I would have to stay here alone," she softly said. "I've been waiting for almost an hour for you to come to me. What took you so long?"

I didn't say anything as I slid under the covers and melted her into my arms. She was dressed as I was, shorts and a t-shirt, but the warmth of her body found its way through to me. I held her gently in my arms and stared at her wondrous face for what seemed an eternity. She never blinked as she stared back. I bent my head forward and touched her lips with mine and the world went away until I felt her scalding tears on my face. Damn, damn, damn, damn, damn!

"I'm afraid," she whispered against my lips.

"Of me?"

"Of us," she replied.

"Don't be. Nothing will happen you don't want. If all you can stand is for me to hold you all night, that's exactly what you'll get. And nothing more." I said, as she settled in my arms.

Sighing softly, she snuggled against me and appeared to go to sleep. I had no idea where this night would lead, if anywhere, but I wasn't about to screw things up by being, shall we say, too forward. If it took me lying here in this position all night without moving, I'd do it. It couldn't be any harder than lying in a muddy ditch, covered with leaves and grass, feeling the leeches biting in places I really didn't want them, waiting for my shot of opportunity.

Sometime shortly before dawn, as my arm continued its numbing, Mila sighed again and rolled over, placing her back to me. I covered us both up again and lay there watching the dawn break over the green hills. My arm hurt like hell, but I said nothing. I just laid there as the tingling grew and then subsided to a dull ache. As the sun broke the horizon, Mila yawned and asked me if I were awake. I kissed the back of her neck and she giggled softly. Slowly, with great deliberation, she rolled back over to face me.

"I slept well. Better than I have in many months. Did you have a good night?" she asked.

I replied by lightly kissing her forehead, then her cheeks and finally, her sweet luscious lips.

"I'll take that as a "yes", she muttered. "We need to go in now and fix Uncle Silvestro some breakfast. He'll be up and about very soon if he hasn't stayed up all night. Sometimes, when he gets his teeth into a problem, he forgets to sleep and eat."

Mila rose and began to gather the bedding and put it away into a chest under the seat of one of the outdoor settees. I hadn't noticed there being storage space there before, but hey–I had been distracted. Once the bedding had been put away, we sent inside and Mila started cooking.

Mario was already there drinking coffee and just grinned when we came in. Mila lightly slapped him on the cheek and signed something I didn't catch. It mattered not to me; he could think what he wished. Mila came over to me and kissed me fully on the lips and melted against me, then grinned and told me to go get dressed. As I turned to go put some clothes on, she slapped me on my butt. Feeling very jubilant, I strolled on down to my room and changed into something more formal than shorts.

By the time I got back into the kitchen, bacon, eggs and toast was waiting for me on a nice china plate along with a steaming cup of coffee. I bailed right in and started eating as if I hadn't eaten in a while. Mario was still grinning, but managed to duck another slap from Mila.

"Buon Giorno, Tutti," Silvestro bellowed as he entered the kitchen.

I may never get used to how loud Silvestro is, but I am going to try real hard, for Mila's sake.

When he sat down at the counter, Mila slid a platter to him with at least a half pound of bacon, half a dozen eggs and four slices of toast on it.

"Am I now on a diet, Niece? This is only enough food for a small child." Silvestro complained.

"You eat that while I prepare more. I have only two hands to feed two grown men with. Manga e' fa' cucco." Mila replied.

Silvestro smiled and commenced eating. "I have discovered more information regarding your blood, but still cannot tell you how it happens. I injected a line of mice with an extract from the blood and am now up to seven generations that exhibit the same traits as you and Mila. I will continue until I either get tired of injecting mice or discover where the trait stops, if it ever does. I would never have believed it would go seven transfers, but it has. I should be able to go fifteen or more today. If they all exhibit the same traits, I shall have my assistant continue that line of research and I'll start something else."

"Whatever you think best, Uncle." Mila said as she slid another platter across the counter to him. "Jason and I are going to check out the nets today. We'll take Mario to run the boat."

"You be careful. Mario, take whatever you need to protect them. Whatever! Capice?" Silvestro stated firmly.

Mario nodded briefly and left the kitchen. Mila gestured toward the stove and raised her eyebrows as she looked at me. I shook my head 'no' and she turned off the heat to the burners. Silvestro finished his morning repast and leaned over to kiss Mila before he left. "Ciao, Belissima. You take care of her, Jason, and bring her back. I still owe her a huge wedding."

I shook his hand as he left for his laboratory and he patted me on the shoulder as he went by. I felt him drop something heavy into my jacket pocket as he passed me by, but made no comment. I followed him into the hallway, but he never looked back. I reached into my jacket pocket and drew out the heavy object. It was a forty-one caliber, stainless steel semi-automatic pistol; one of the best you can buy. It has a fourteen round magazine plus one in the chamber for a total of fifteen shots. It kicks like a mule and if you don't pay attention, it'll whack you in the head from its recoil. It just might come in handy.

CHAPTER IV

"Mario, would you please cast off the bow line?" Mila yelled, as she pushed the throttle just a bit to slacken the line. Mario tossed the bow line onto the deck and kicked the boat away from the dock with his foot. Mila shoved the throttle a bit harder and we were under way. I sure hoped she knew what she was doing because this boat was twice as large as I had ever tried to maneuver. My little sailboat had only been blessed with a thirty-horse diesel and this monster had twin inboards that would make a race car envious. Me, I'm not too fond of stinkboats in the first place. I prefer the smell of the wind driven water vapors to the odor of diesel.

Mario and Mila were conversing too swiftly for me to follow their signs, so I made myself comfortable on the railing and just let the wind blow in my face. We were heading out to the bay where Mario figured the nets were most likely to be damaged. Mila was busy piloting the boat while Mario was looking at the maps and guiding her. I moved myself forward and decided to climb to the top and sit in the lookout's chair. I'd be further away from the noise and smell of those big engines, plus I could see farther into the distance and into the clear blue water.

We motored out of the bay and turned right toward the sheltered cove as I climbed up to the lookout's chair. I settled in and belted myself into a comfortable position. Taking the monocular out of its case, I began to adjust the lenses to fit my vision. Just as I got it into focus, we slowed down to a crawl. Looking over the side, I could see Mario and Mila were having a heated discussion about something. They both "talked" so fast with their hands, I couldn't keep up, so I picked up the phone at my side and pushed the call button. Mila answered with a curt "What?"

I asked if I needed to come down and separate them before they drew blood and she laughed and said "No, Mario just wants to be too cautious and I don't. There's nothing to be cautious for. If the nets are damaged, it won't be because of anything but the sea. Stay up there and enjoy the view." She hung up the phone and I went back to scanning the sea for whatever I could find.

We picked up speed again and I settled back into a comfortable position to keep watching a pair of dolphins cavorting in the sea in front of us. It was a beautiful day for being out on the sea and a wonderful day to be alive and in love.

The two dolphins kept up their game of riding our bow waves for another ten minutes and then suddenly disappeared. That caught my attention and I began scanning in earnest for what might have driven them off. I looked straight down to see what Mila might be doing and was surprised to see what looked like a submarine just off to our right and almost parallel to us. I shouted to Mila, but she couldn't hear over the engines roar. Picking up the phone, I called down to "Captain" Mila and told her to look over the side to the right. She stepped to the rail and looked over. The dark shape veered suddenly toward us and she immediately ran to the wheel and turned it rapidly to the left. For a few seconds, I thought the sub would ram us, but it veered off to the right and appeared to be diving.

"What the hell was that?" Mila yelled into the phone.

"Looked like a sub from up here. It was too big to be anything else. There aren't any whales that big in this part of the Mediterranean and it was too fast to be a whale anyway," I replied.

Mario had disappeared down into the cabins and now reappeared with a box that looked suspiciously like an ammo box. Prying off the lid, he pulled the paper off the top and exposed the grenades packed inside. When Mario comes prepared, he comes prepared. I thought it best for me to stay up high so I could warn them if the sub returned and told Mila so. She and Mario agreed.

Mario climbed up to just below my chair and handed me six of the grenades which I stashed in the cooler box under the seat. If it was a sub and it threatened us, I could at least ring its bell enough to cause them some worry and maybe change their course. I kept a close watch on the sea close to us and as far as I could tell, the sub had gone completely. I unbuckled and leaned way out to check closer underneath us. The sea immediately below us was darker, but at first I thought it was only our shadow until I realized the sun was too low for our shadow to be that close to us.

I pushed the call button and when Mila answered, I told her to make a hard right turn and then return to our previous course. When she asked why, I told her. She signaled to Mario and turned the boat to the right. We made a complete circle before we straightened out and all the while I watched the dark shape below us. It made a move to the right, then resumed course when we straightened out again. That wasn't a whale down there.

I made a few calculations in my head, pulled the pin on two grenades and made my tosses. Mario and Mila were watching as I threw them in the direction we were traveling, spacing them about thirty yards apart. When they went off, we could hear the vibration and feel it in the body of the boat. I sure hoped the sub got the message we weren't to be fooled with. Mistake number one.

When the foam died down enough to see below us again, the dark shape was not there. I knew I hadn't hurt it, the grenades didn't go deep enough and they were too small to damage a metal sub that deep, so I figured the grenades had scared them off. Mistake number two.

Leaning out as far left and then as far right as I could, I scanned below us. Nothing. I signed Mila to make a full circle to the right again so I could see better below us. Damn! The dark shape was immediately below us and getting bigger. I clenched my fist and jerked my arm up and down then pointed straight ahead. Mila got the message and pushed the throttles full forward while turning the wheel hard left. Good thing she did. That damned sub came up to the surface right where we had been and splashed down again like a breaching whale. They had tried to ram us from below and we just barely got away.

While Mila and I were running away, Mario had been busy doing what he does best—being prepared. When I looked down, he had already gotten a rocket launcher out of his stash and was aiming at the sub. The sub tried to do an emergency dive and almost made it. Mario's rocket round was either very lucky or he was a hell of a shot. That rocket round hit their periscope and blew it off into the water. They could seal it off and they wouldn't sink, but they would be partially blind now and either would have to locate us by sonar or surface and open a hatch to see us. I thought sure they would go away now. Mistake number three.

Mila started making zigzags in the water and varied her speed while I kept a close watch on the sea around us. I didn't know what Mario was doing, but I'm sure he was thinking up something new to do about our predicament. Mila had decided to return to the dock, I'm sure, because we were now going the opposite direction we had been traveling.

For about twenty minutes I thought we had it made. The dark shadow coming from below and behind us changed my mind. It sure looked like our buddy was after us again. I called down to Mila who had a short conversation with Mario. He went back down into the cabin and disappeared from sight. That shadow was catching us and I told Mila so. Just then, Mario came back up on deck carrying a large object on his right shoulder. It looked like a metal drum of some kind. He screwed something into the top of it and rolled it to the stern of the boat.

Mario stood at the stern and watched the shadow get closer. He turned a dial of some sort on the drum and pushed it off the rear into our wake. He then turned and picked up an umbrella and opened it with a grin. It suddenly made sense when the sea behind us erupted and sent a huge spray of water upwards, completely wetting everyone except Mario. After the drenching stopped, Mario put away the umbrella and inspected the sea once again. The shadow that had been coming toward us was now stopped and appeared to be getting deeper, rather than shallower.

Mila and Mario signed a bit and we continued on our way back to the dock. We still kept a sharp lookout for anything under the water, but it seemed we had either damaged or, at least, discouraged whoever was following us. Docking was anti-climatic and after tying the boat up, we went on home. Silvestro might have a friend somewhere who could check out what or who that sub might have belonged to. Mila had saved the GPS coordinates where we had dropped the depth charge over the stern. I hoped we hadn't killed anyone, but having them sit on the bottom for a while just might make them think twice before they tried to come after us again.

Mila and Mario were certain the sub had a lot to do with the nets being damaged and I was in agreement with them. What intrigued me was where the sharks had come from. This area isn't their normal range. Could they have been captured and then released here or lured in some way. Silvestro got on the phone and started talking. When he does that, one might as well go away and do something useful. I guess that's a good thing for a scientist.

Mila and Mario were already in the kitchen cooking up something to eat. I sliced up some bread and spread it with soft cheese; Mila put prosciutto on the slices along with pepperoncini, some lettuce and slices of ripe olives. She then slid them into a small toaster oven and the aroma was delightful. The taste was even better. I think I could get used to her way of cooking. I sure am hoping to eat a lot more of her cooking.

Mario, of course, never said a word. He just ate four of the delicious sandwiches and drank three beers. After he belched, he grinned, left the kitchen and closed the door behind him. Mila said nothing about him leaving, just pulled off her apron and rounded the counter to where I was sitting with my last half sandwich in one hand and a glass of milk in the other. Taking my face in her hands, she kissed me and my heart stopped. The milk must have spilled when I tried to put it down and I don't remember what I did with the sandwich. When you get kissed like that, everything else stops being important.

"Mila," I mumbled. "What about your uncle?"

"Shut up and pay attention to me." Mila said as she looked me in the eye and smiled.

So I did.

Paying attention to Mila has become my favorite thing to do and she seems to like it too. We paid attention to each other until we got tired of standing up and decided to move to the parlor. The parlor was much more private and besides, the floors were parquet and we would be able to hear anyone coming. In addition, there was a large very overstuffed couch in one corner of the room quietly beckoning us as we entered the parlor. That's all it got to do because Mario came running down the hall and burst through the door. He signed rapidly to Mila, who immediately took on a look of horror. They took off running; Mila stopped and yelled for me to follow, then took off again. I followed as best as I could but they had a head start and were fast on their feet. Once the path was clear to me they were heading to the lab, I slowed down a bit and arrived just in time to help Mila give artificial respiration to her uncle. In between breaths, I told

Mario to dial the emergency number and hand Mila the phone when someone answered.

Of a sudden, Silvestro gasped, groaned and tried to roll over. Mila stopped him and told him to wait for the paramedics.

"Oh my. Did I pass out again? I must learn not to use that chemical without a mask." Silvestro said. "I'm really fine. It was only an overdose of the ether I was using to dissolve a small amount of oil out of an experimental compound."

"So you say, uncle, but let's be sure and let these fine people do their job" Mila said.

While we were busy with Silvestro, the paramedics had arrived and had already started laying out what they needed to use to check out Silvestro.

Begrudgingly, he allowed the fuss to continue until they wanted to take him to the hospital for further tests. That's when he put his foot down and told them they were free to go bother someone else. Mila spoke to the one in charge and seemed satisfied her uncle was going to be alright and then thanked them for their service and quick response. They gathered their equipment, stowed it and left as quickly as they came.

"I'm going to beat you to within an inch of your life if you do that again to me!" Mila shouted in her uncle's face. Sheepishly, he promised to always wear a mask when using ether, no matter how small an amount it may be. Mila hugged him, apologized for shouting at him and they went to the kitchen, arm in arm.

Mario looked at me, shrugged and turned his hands up as if to say "what'cha gonna do" and followed them toward the kitchen. I fell in behind, shaking my head. "What a crazy family." I thought, "And I'm going to join them. Life is getting interesting."

It wasn't long before the smell from the kitchen wafted back to Mario and I. Mario rubbed his belly, smiled and ambled toward the kitchen with me, starting to drool, right behind. I'm not sure which one of them had cooked the meal and Mario and I really didn't care, it smelled so good. Neither of us asked what the casserole consisted of; we just settled down at the table and made pigs of ourselves. Both Mila and Silvestro were jabbering away in that musical language I was beginning to understand. It seems they were discussing something about the hall in town and food lists, guests and many other things I got lost in. I figured when I was supposed to know they'd tell me. Besides Mario and I were busy with casserole, wine and bread. If there was a minor reason to stay here at Silvestro's, it would be the food those two could cook up.

If I'm not careful I'm going to be as big as a house in a few months. 'Oh well, it could be a lot worse." I thought. "Mila could be beautiful, smart and a lousy cook." Then I thought about what I'd eaten so far and hadn't gained a pound. It could be that this is the norm for Mila and me; forever young and trim. Not a bad thought.

"Jason, come to the kitchen and tell me what this needs." Mila's voice summoned. I, of course, complied. I could not imagine what input I might provide, but I was more than willing to give it a shot just to be near Mila.

Silvestro was sitting at the small table when I got there and seemed disinterested in the cooking part of the meal. Not me. The aroma here in the kitchen was definitely more enticing. "What have you cooked up that smells so fine, Mila?" I asked.

"Taste it and tell me what it needs." She replied.

I took the spoon she handed me, blew on it and slurped the liquid. I, for the life of me, could not tell that it needed anything to be added. "Mila, all it needs is for me to be around this delightful concoction before Mario gets to it. May I have a large portion of whatever this is?"

"No, tell me if it needs salt, oregano, pepper or what." She insisted.

"I told you all it needs is for me to get a large portion before that big food vacuum gets here and there's only a tablespoon left. It tastes perfectly fine to me. Now quit arguing and feed me."

With a big grin, she handed a large bowlful to me and Mario's hand suddenly appeared over my shoulder to grab the bowl before I could touch it. But it was ok because Mila had cooked enough to feed an army and another bowl came rapidly.

Tossing a loaf of bread on the small table was Mila's idea of setting the table. Silvestro got a much larger bowl than either of ours and Mila filled it to the brim. The stew she had made was as good as any I had ever tasted, so I went back for seconds, slightly behind Mario. Mario grabbed another loaf of bread, which Silvestro immediately took a third of. Staying even with those two turned into a full time job, but I think I managed pretty well.

After serving us three, Mila took a bowl of the stew and pulled a chair up to sit with us and compete with all three for some bread. She won each time and forced Mario back to the cupboard for another loaf. Setting the new loaf on the table, Mario reached back to pull his chair forward and lost one end piece of the new loaf. You have to be fast at this table. Silvestro laughed and reached for more bread, but failed because Mario had stuck the remainder of the loaf in his bowl, forcing Silvestro to go to the cupboard. Me? I hoarded what bread I had and continued to the bottom of my bowl.

CHAPTER V

"Mario, I need for you and I to go shopping for a ring set. You said you knew some jewelers and I think it's past time to formalize my feelings for Mila. When can we go and how do we get there?" I asked.

Mario signed-'now and in the car.' Mario is always succinct in his 'speech.' He got up from the table, checked his shoulder holster, his ankle holster and the holster in the small of his back. He then checked the knives in his sleeves and the one at the back of his neck and 'said lets go' in his inimitable sign language.

"Mila, Mario and I are going to town for a few things. Would you like us to bring you something back? Ask Silvestro if he needs anything." I asked when I stuck my head into the kitchen where they were cleaning up from lunch.

"Yes, I would like a ring set of no more than ½ karat in platinum for the wedding ring and the same for the engagement ring, both in a size seven, if you please." She replied sweetly.

"There's just no surprising you, is there, Miss Big Ears." I retorted.

"If you wouldn't talk so loud, I wouldn't hear so well, Mr. Big Mouth." She said with a big smile. "And Silvestro said to go by the Hall, Mario knows where, and reserve it for next Saturday. We need to formally introduce you to the townsfolks."

"In that case, now that you know about the ring set, would you like to come and pick it out yourself?"

"No. I want you to decide what looks best on me."

Mario laughed and signed for me to come along. It was early in the afternoon, but who knew how long it might take. It might take more than this one trip, depending on many things. Hopefully, I could find just the right one today, but I doubted it. I had something specific in mind and it might take a jeweler some time to make a set. Only one way to find out and that was to go look.

Mario, once again, took a circuitous path toward the town, but by now I trusted him implicitly. Either he knew all the best roads, or he was dodging anything that might be a trap. In the town, we stopped at a building that looked more like a pizzeria than a jewelry shop. Mario told me to wait in the car and went inside. It was a pleasant day and I spent my time watching the people go by.

Mario returned with a small man carrying a black attaché case. The man gestured for me to get in the back seat with him. I complied and he opened the attaché case to show the most dazzling array of diamonds I had ever seen. I examined many lovely sets of rings but couldn't find exactly what I wanted. I told the man two of the sets were close but not what I wanted. He took out a pad and I showed him the set with the setting on the engagement ring I liked, but the wedding ring was off. I then showed him the wedding ring I liked, but it was gold and not platinum.

"If I can get the wedding ring in platinum, will you buy?" He asked.

"Yes. Is the engagement ring platinum?" I asked. "Both must be platinum, not white gold."

"Of course, Signore. My job is to satisfy you. And the payment will be charge or cash?" He asked.

"I deal only in cash. This ring set is for Mila, Silvestro---Mario, what is Silvestro's last name?" I asked.

Mario took out a pad and wrote "Duina." I took the paper and told the jeweler who the ring set was for, Mila, Silvestro Duina's niece.

He laughed and told me he was well acquainted with both of them and would give me the best possible price. "And the size, Sir?"

"Seven"

"They will be ready in six days. Will you pick them up, or do you wish them delivered?"

"I'd best pick them up. Things sometimes get in the way and I never know whether I'll be there at any given time. Mario will have me here on time, like it or not."

Mario thought that was funny and slapped me on the back just hard enough to stagger me. He is one big man that knows his strength.

What we did not know was that we were being watched and being reported on by two different men from two different directions. We would find out later just who hired them and why. They were very good at surveillance as neither I nor Mario caught on; or it could have been because we were preoccupied with the rings. Things like that can get one hurt. It certainly taught me a lesson.

Our next stop would be the Hall to make arrangements for the rental on Saturday next week. Since today was Thursday, I was sure Mila meant Saturday next, not this coming weekend. She did say next Saturday not this Saturday.

Arriving at the Hall, Mario got out of the car, but motioned for me to stay where I was while he went up the stairs to the large main doors. Once he got to the top, he turned and motioned for me to come up too. He kept his back to the doors and once I got there, he signed for me to look over my left shoulder at the café across the street. Only one person was at an outside table and appeared to be reading a newspaper and drinking coffee. We turned and went inside. Mario kept the door open a crack and smiled when he looked out the crack.

"The man at the table hurriedly left and got in the black car that has been following us." Mario told me. "The car belongs to the Verducci's and I'll bet the men have been following us all morning. It makes me wonder why they are following us. Is it because of you specifically, or the fact that you and the Duina's are close?"

Good question to be asked, I thought. I told Mario I couldn't believe it was me in particular, as no one knew me in this part of the world, so it had to be because of the Duina's. I could see he was thinking and finally agreed it was because of the relationship I had with the Duina's. It never crossed my mind that it might be because of Mario. He was so formidable and scary; I just couldn't believe someone would try to harm him. How wrong I was.

We made the arrangements for the Hall with the priest in charge and were proceeding back to our car to go home. When Mario stepped out the door, a burst of automatic weapons fire hit the big wooden doors of the Hall, barely missing Mario who had dropped and rolled back inside. He immediately reopened the doors in time to see that same black car that had followed us earlier speeding away to the south. He shrugged his shoulders as if to say 'so much for that'. He picked up his hat and stuck his fingers through the holes in the crown and with a grin he wriggled them at me, and then signed he needed a new hat. Waving me outside, we got in the car and on the way home I bought him a much better new hat to wear. As we passed a farmer with a donkey cart, he threw his old hat out the window and the farmer picked it up. I looked back and the farmer was putting the hat on his donkey. Didn't look bad from here.

Mario wasn't at all talkative on the way home and he had that "I'm doing some serious thinking" look on his face. I'd have bet the farm that it concerned Verducci's men and when we pulled in to the driveway to put the car away, we went around the lab to the left instead of into the parking area we always used which told me I was right. I didn't really know what he was up to, but I'm betting he's going for some better ammunition to "settle" with the guys that tried to kill him.

Better ammunition hardly describes what Mario put in the car and what he put on himself. He must have gained eighty pounds himself and two hundred for the car. Mario was now ready to smack a grizzly in the face and take away his salmon. I am definitely awed at what Mario has thought up and I'm so looking forward to this particular dance. Verducci had best not interfere himself or "look out Sally" as they say.

Mario asked if I was going to go with him or "stand there with my hands in my pockets?" The car door slammed on my side before he got sat down. At that point, he handed me a box of grenades, an AK-47 and two pistols. One of the pistols was a Glock 9mm and the other was a stainless steel Colt 44 Magnum. He tossed two boxes of ammo for each gun into my lap and away we went, hardly giving me time to buckle up. Both pistols were loaded so I didn't have to try putting shells in them while traveling over these cobblestone roads. I checked the double magazines for the AK and, of course, they were full.

Wending our way through the back streets was a piece of cake for this Italian behemoth. Maybe I've forgotten to mention just how big this dude is. He's well over six feet tall, with shoulders like a NFL linebacker, biceps bigger than my leg and pretty much all muscle; except for his mind. That part of him is like a steel trap and faster than a speeding bullet. Mario surprises me just how light on his feet he is and just how fast he is. He's extremely protective of the Duina family, but most especially Mila. I'm sure he would take on a charging elephant if it meant Mila was in danger.

Mario gestured with his right hand that we were almost there, get ready. I jacked a round into the chamber of the 9mm and the AK, rolled my window down and prepared for the worst. When we rounded the corner, the two guys that had followed us were outside the villa washing the black sedan they had used to follow us. Mario took two grenades out of the box, steered with his left hand, pulled the pins with his teeth and tossed them through the window of that black

Mercedes. Might I mention the window wasn't open at the time and the grenades went out through my window into the other car?

Whipping the car around, Mario let me have a turn at the two gorillas. The Glock spat twice and the nearest one went down with two 9mm's in his backside. The other one got an AK round through both legs just below hip level. Neither of them would be walking well for a long time. Mario stopped the car out of the smoke from the Mercedes and walked over to them both and fired one round adjacent to their heads. That was a message they would remember and take to heart if they had any sense.

I got out of the car, walked over to the two lying there on the ground and told them both in my halting Italian to leave. I said France is nice, Germany is better and Norway, Denmark or Sweden would be best. No second chances would be given. The next time would definitely be fatal. They both agreed leaving would be a good idea and they would be doing so at the first opportunity. I said "Gratzie" and got back in our car. Mario gave me a high five and chirped the tires as we left. I wondered how long it would be before Verducci would have someone try again.

It was a nice quiet drive back to the laboratory/home. Thinking real hard about what had just happened; it dawned on me they were after Mario, not me. Mario had been protecting the Duina family for many years successfully and if he was out of the picture it would be much easier to get to Silvestro.

"Mario, I think they were after you, not me. They can't get to Silvestro with you in the way. You're too good a bodyguard for them to succeed. What say we go visit Verducci in his house? Beard the lion in his den, so to speak."

Mario replied that it was impossibility because there were too many guards, besides his house was on an island and the only approach was by water. That got me to thinking about the new type of Scuba gear that used the moisture in your breath to generate oxygen and didn't leave any bubbles. I'd have to look into seeing where to buy such. In the meantime, just let the grey matter work on a plan after getting Mario to describe what he knew about Verducci's island fortress. I sometimes did my best thinking while asleep. And after today, I sure could use some sleep.

It took longer to unload the car once we got back than it did to load it. All the stuff Mario put in the car had to be repacked in their protective cases and put away in such a manner that it was still quickly accessible when needed. Mario is nothing but neat when it comes to his weaponry. If I didn't do it correctly, he fussed at me.

Walking into the kitchen our noses were assaulted by a myriad of wonderful smells. Mila must be cooking again. She can make so much out of almost nothing, it's amazing. Just a little pasta, some garlic and seasonings, a touch of sausage and bread fresh from the ovens and there's a meal fit for a king or me. One can gain weight just by smelling the odors emanating from the stove. It surprises me no one is gaining inches on this diet, not even Mila.

I hugged Mila from behind, kissed her on the neck and she immediately spun around to really kiss me. She wrapped her arms around my neck and wouldn't let go for quite a while. When she did, she had tears in her eyes. When I asked why she was crying, she hit me on the arm and said, "You were in danger and I was worried about you."

"Have you forgotten who I am and what getting hurt applies to me?" I asked.

She had a puzzled look on her face and replied, "No matter, you were in danger and I was afraid for you."

I had forgotten that Mila was not always logical so I let it go and said I was sorry for worrying her. I reminded her Mario was with me and took care of me very well. Not a scratch to be seen anywhere on either of us. That placated her and she went back to the stove to continue cooking. I glanced at Mario and he just grinned and gestured he was going to go wash up. I assumed Silvestro was in his lab and decided to go chat with him about the rebreather scuba gear. Maybe he knew where I could buy a set. I knew it wouldn't be locally, but with his contacts, he surely knew where to buy rebreathers. I also must remember to question Silvestro regarding Verducci's island fortress in case he knew something Mario did not.

I asked some of the technicians where Silvestro might be and no one knew. That seemed strange to me, so I went back to the kitchen to ask Mila if she had any idea where her uncle might be at this time of day if he wasn't in his lab. She didn't know for sure, but he had said he was going to town and assumed it had something to do with this coming weekend at the Hall. I had been looking forward to this weekend. I like meeting new people and my Italian language skills have improved since I got here, so I shouldn't have too much trouble. Besides, everyone I'd met so far made allowances for my crude grammar and diction. I had to insist on them correcting me as it seems they think it impolite to correct someone's speech. I put it to them as a way to assist a poor ignorant American and that usually sufficed to get them to assist me in learning. The learning process was progressing nicely and I was becoming more fluent with every conversation. That needed to occur if I were to be a part of this family.

Time flew by so swiftly that the day to announce arrived and we all went to the Hall to announce our engagement. Only that never occurred. It turned out to be the biggest wedding this town had ever seen. I had dressed in my wedding suit expecting to only announce our engagement at this time but I had been outfoxed by my gorgeous bride. Everything had been prepared ahead of time and I only had to sign one paper and the priest started the ceremony. To my surprise it had been arranged by Silvestro. He had so much influence he bypassed many rules that normally occurred.

My heart jumped two or three hurdles when I saw Mila enter the Hall. God, she is so beautiful in that white wedding gown. I almost cried, I was so happy and surprised. I don't remember much of what was said, just responded where needed. We exchanged rings, we kissed and then we were married. Just that simple. I had teared up and Mila was crying profusely. Silvestro and Mario were trying to console her and she started laughing and told them she was crying because she was so very happy.

"I never thought I would find such a man and of all places to find him, in the middle of the ocean while fishing. I have never known anyone who could top this man in anything. He's mine and I'm going to keep him forever. So there!"

I couldn't keep from laughing myself and then Mario and Silvestro joined us along with most of the citizenry in the Hall. The wedding party departed the Hall to go to the outdoor pavilion where the wine and food were. The party lasted well into the night, but Mila and I escaped around one a.m. to go to her boat. Mario and Silvestro had stocked it with pretty much whatever we'd need for a month or so.

We had no idea where we were going, just spending the next part of our life together alone. We still had much to learn about each other, but we both thought it would be best if we did it without anyone pushing us in any particular direction. We launched the boat about two a.m. as quiet as we could, but Mario had other ideas. He set off enough fireworks for a fourth of July celebration and woke up the whole town that had not attended the wedding. So much for a quiet retreat.

We turned the boat east to head first to Greece, then to maybe Turkey just because Mila had never been to either place. Nor had I, so why not. The wind was blowing from the west so we used the sails as long as the wind would blow. We had plenty of diesel in case we needed to motor. I think back on that day and felt more satisfied than I ever had before. Looking forward to tomorrow plus.